BLACK VOICES
ON BRITAIN

More anthologies available from
Macmillan Collector's Library

No Place Like Home ed. Michèle Mendelssohn

Why Friendship Matters ed. Michèle Mendelssohn

On Your Marks ed. Martin Polley

Our Place in Nature ed. Zachary Seager

The Art of Solitude ed. Zachary Seager

Food for Thought ed. Annie Gray

The Joy of Walking ed. Suzy Cripps

BLACK VOICES
ON BRITAIN

Selected Writings

Edited and introduced by
HAKIM ADI

MACMILLAN COLLECTOR'S LIBRARY

This collection first published 2022 by Macmillan Collector's Library
an imprint of Pan Macmillan
The Smithson, 6 Briset Street, London EC1M 5NR
EU representative: Macmillan Publishers Ireland Ltd, 1st Floor,
The Liffey Trust Centre, 117–126 Sheriff Street Upper,
Dublin 1, DO1 YC43
Associated companies throughout the world
www.panmacmillan.com

ISBN 978-1-5290-7261-7

Selection, introduction and author biographies © Hakim Adi 2022

'London' by W. E. B. Du Bois published by *The Crisis*, August 1911, and
reproduced with their permission.

'Memoirs of the Life of Boston King, A Black Preacher' by Boston King is reproduced
with the help of the Antislavery Literature Project, Arizona State University.

Thanks to Nicole-Rachelle Moore at The British Library for her help in
supplying a copy of *Hard Truth*.

1 3 5 7 9 8 6 4 2

A CIP catalogue record for this book is available from the British Library.

Casing design and endpaper pattern by Andrew Davidson
Typeset by Jouve (UK), Milton Keynes
Printed and bound in China by Imago

Visit www.panmacmillan.com to read more about all our books
and to buy them.

Contents

Introduction

HAKIM ADI

What was it like to be a Black person in Britain in the eighteenth or nineteenth century? A difficult question to answer perhaps, since it was undoubtedly dependent on whether an individual was enslaved or free, rich or poor, male or female, literate or illiterate. It also depended on whether someone was born in Britain or arrived as a colonial 'subject' from the Caribbean or Africa, or as a fugitive from North America. It may be said that there were as many experiences as there were visitors and residents, and there were certainly thousands of both. Unfortunately, although we know something about the lives of Black people during this period, we know very little about what they thought of their experience of living in Britain. Some were literate, but many others left no record. What we have are merely the published writings of a few men and even fewer women.

Today we might think that the existence of racism, a consequence of enslavement and colonialism, produced some common experiences. Ignatius Sancho, the eighteenth-century African composer and distinguished man of letters, spent almost his entire life in Britain, but once referred to himself as 'only a lodger – and hardly that', as if to emphasize that he still didn't feel he belonged. Others, such as James Gronniosaw, an African prince who had formerly been enslaved, 'expected to find nothing but goodness, gentleness and meekness in this Christian Land', and was rather disappointed by the reality. Even Mary Seacole, the celebrated heroine of the Crimea War, recalled that of her first impressions of Britain in the early nineteenth century, 'some of the most vivid of my recollections are the efforts of the London street-boys to poke fun at my and my companion's complexion.'

Yet many celebrated African Americans who came to Britain not much later remarked on how free of racism their experiences in Britain were compared to those they had left behind in the 'land of the free and the home of the brave.' The fugitive Frederick Douglass wrote of his experiences at an English stately home, 'When the door was opened, I walked in, on an equal footing with my white fellow-citizens, and from all I could see, I had as much attention paid me by the servants that showed us through the house, as any with a paler skin.' William Wells Brown, another African American fugitive, remarked, 'the prejudice which I have experienced on all and every occasion in the United States, and to some extent on board the *Canada*, vanished as soon as I set foot on the soil of Britain.'

Africans and those of African descent have been visiting Britain for many centuries, probably for a thousand years before the Roman conquerors. Yet it is only in relatively recent times that we have written examples of their views and concerns, and few of these are accounts of their experiences of Britain. This anthology aims to present some of these experiences as recorded by those of African, Caribbean and African American heritage, who resided in or visited Britain. Some of the authors included – such as the abolitionist and writer Olaudah Equiano, Mary Seacole and African American scholar–activist W. E. B. Du Bois – are now well-known personalities, widely recognized for their wider contributions to society, as well as for their literary prowess. Others, like Mary Prince, held as a slave in London in the early 1830s, the editor S. J. Celestine Edwards and John Ocansey, a visitor from the Gold Coast, may be less well known, but their observations and recollections are equally fascinating.

What all these authors have in common is that they described their experiences of Britain in their writing. Some extracts are taken from well-known autobiographies such as *The Interesting Narrative of the Life of Olaudah Equiano, or Gustavas Vassa, the African* and Seacole's *Wonderful Adventures of Mrs. Seacole in Many Lands,* but also included are extracts from works of fiction, such as J. E. Casely Hayford's *Ethiopia Unbound: Studies in Race Emancipation* and Celestine Edward's satirical work *Hard Truth,* which presents an entirely fictional account of a discussion between Christ and the Devil. Also included are articles published in the press from Du Bois and Sarah Parker Remond, as well as letters from Ignatius Sancho.

One of the obvious characteristics shared by these writers is that they were all published. Although some were first published in the United States, the majority were published in Britain – itself a significant achievement. It is one thing to have something to say, yet another to find someone who is willing to publish it. What is more, several of the publications were clearly undertaken for overtly political reasons, including the work of Olaudah Equiano, James Gronniosaw, Mary Prince and Ignatius Sancho. Although Sancho's letters were published posthumously, this was evidently done to show 'that an untutored African may possess abilities equal to an European', an aim as openly political as that connected with the publications of the life histories of the other three who were formerly enslaved. Gronniosaw and Prince dictated their autobiographies to scribes, but Equiano was clearly a talented, largely self-taught writer – one of the first to develop a new literary genre, the 'slave narrative'. This form of abolitionist propaganda was then further developed by several African American writers featured here, including Frederick Douglass, Harriet Jacobs and William Wells Brown, who, like Equiano, wrote best-selling autobiographies.

Some of the writing featured here does not fall into any established genre, and its publication is thus even more significant and fascinating. This is particularly the case with A. B. C. Merriman-Labor's satirical sketch of *Britons Through Negro Spectacles* and the fictionalized dialogue between Christ and the Devil regarding the ills of Britain's racism and imperialism in *Hard Truth*; this book's approach is all the more surprising given that its author, generally considered to be S. J. Celestine Edwards, was a devout Christian evangelist and a lay preacher.

Whatever their differences or similarities, all of the individuals included tell us something significant and thought-provoking about their experiences of life in Britain.

BLACK VOICES
ON BRITAIN

JAMES GRONNIOSAW

Born into royalty in the kingdom of Bornu (today northern Nigeria), James Albert Gronniosaw (*c.* 1705–1775) became the first African writer in England when his *Narrative*, or autobiography, was published in Bath in 1772. Tricked into enslavement, he was transported to Barbados and then New York, where he was freed after the death of his owner. He later served in the navy and army before arriving in England, where he married a widowed silk weaver. His *Narrative* was recorded for him 'by the elegant pen of a young lady from Leominster' for her private satisfaction, but subsequently published 'to serve Albert and his distressed family.' These narratives were autobiographical accounts, which related at first hand the experience of slavery and liberation. This extract presents evidence of Gronniosaw's strong Calvinistic faith, his first impressions of England and his future wife, as well as the impoverished existence, unemployment and many challenges he faced.

A Narrative of the Most Remarkable Particulars in the Life of James Albert Ukawsaw Gronniosaw, an African Prince, as Related by Himself

I was then worth about thirty pounds, but I never regarded money in the least, nor would I tarry for my prize-money least I should lose my chance of going to England. I went with the Spanish prisoners to Spain; and came to Old-England with the English prisoners. I cannot describe my joy when we were within sight of Portsmouth. But I was astonished when we landed to hear the inhabitants of that place curse and swear and otherwise profane. I expected to find nothing but goodness, gentleness and meekness in this Christian land, I then suffered great perplexities of mind.

I enquired if any serious Christian people resided there, the woman I made this enquiry of, answered me in the affirmative; and added that she was one of them. I was heartily glad to hear her say so. I thought I could give her my whole heart; she kept a public house. I deposited with her all the money that I had not an immediate occasion for; as I thought it would be safer with her.—It was 25 guineas but 6 of them I desired her to lay out to the best advantage, to buy me some shirts, a hat and some other necessaries. I made her a present of a very handsome large looking glass that I brought with me from Martinico, in order to recompence her for the trouble I had given her. I must do this woman the justice to acknowledge that she did lay out some little for my use, but the 19 guineas and part of the 6 guineas with my watch, she would not return, but denied that I ever gave it her.

I soon perceived that I was got among bad people, who defrauded me of my money and watch; and that all my promised happiness was blasted. I had no friend but GOD and I prayed to him earnestly. I could scarcely believe it possible that the place where so many eminent Christians had lived and preached could abound with so much wickedness and deceit. I thought it worse than *Sodom* (considering the great advantage they have). I cried like a child, and that almost continually: at length GOD heard my prayers, and raised me a friend indeed.

This publican had a brother who lived on Portsmouth-Common, his wife was a very serious good woman.—When she heard of the treatment I had met with, she came and enquired into my real situation, and was greatly troubled at the ill usage I had received, and took me home to her own house. I began now to rejoice, and my prayer was turned into praise. She made use of all the arguments in her power to prevail on her who had wronged me to return my watch and money, but it was to no purpose, as she had given me no receipt, and I had nothing to shew for it, I could not demand it. My good friend was excessively angry with her, and obliged her to give me back four guineas, which she said she gave me out of charity; though in fact it was my own and much more. She would have employed some rougher means to oblige her to give up my money, but I would not suffer her, let it go, says I, "My GOD is in heaven." Still I did not mind my loss in the least; all that grieved me was, that I had been disappointed in finding some Christian friends, with whom I hoped to enjoy a little sweet and comfortable society.

I thought the best method that I could take now, was to go to London, and find out Mr. Whitefield, who was the only living soul I knew in England, and get him to direct me how to procure a living without being troublesome to any person. I took leave of my Christian friend at Portsmouth, and went in the stage to London. A creditable tradesman in the city, who went up with me in the stage, offered to shew me the way to Mr. Whitefield's tabernacle. Knowing that I was a perfect stranger, I thought it very kind, and accepted his offer; but he obliged me to give him half a crown for going with me, and likewise insisted on my giving him five shillings more for conducting me to Dr. Gifford's meeting.

I began now to entertain a very different idea of the inhabitants of England, than what I had figured to myself before I came among them. Mr. Whitefield received me very friendly, was heartily glad to see me, and directed me to a proper place to board and lodge in Petticoat lane, till he could think of some way to settle me in, and paid for my lodging, and all my expences. The morning after I came to my new lodging, as I was at breakfast with the gentlewoman of the house, I heard the noise of some looms over our heads; I enquired what it was, she told me a person was weaving silk. I expressed a great desire to see it, and asked if I might? She told me she would go up with me, and she was sure I should be very welcome. She was as good as her word, and as soon as we entered the room, the person that was weaving looked about, and smiled upon us, and I loved her from that moment. She asked me many questions; and I in return talked a great deal to her. I found she was a member of Mr. Allen's meeting, and I begun to entertain a good opinion of her, though I was almost afraid to indulge this inclination, least she should prove like all the rest I had met with at Portsmouth, &c. and which had almost given me a dislike to all white women. But after a short acquaintance I had the happiness to find she was very different, and quite sincere, and I was not without hopes that she entertained some esteem for me . . . We often went together to hear Dr. Gifford, and as I had always a propensity to relieve every object in distress as far as I was able, I used to give all that complained to me, sometimes half-a-guinea at a time, as I did not understand the real value of it; this gracious good woman took great pains to correct and advise me in that and many other respects.

After I had been in London about six weeks, I was recommended to the notice of some of my late master Mr. Freelandhouse's acquaintance, who had heard him speak frequently of me, I was much persuaded by them to go to Holland. My master lived there before he bought me, and used to speak of me so respectfully among his friends there, that it raised in them a curiosity to see me; particularly the gentlemen engaged in the ministry, who expressed a desire to hear my experience and examine me. I found that it was my good old master's design that I should have gone if he had lived; for which reason I resolved upon going to Holland, and informed my dear friend Mr. Whitefield of my intention; he was much averse to my going at first, but after I gave him my reasons appeared very well satisfied. I likewise informed my Betty (the good woman that I have mentioned above) of my determination to go to Holland, and I told her that I believed she was to be my wife; and if it was the LORD's will I desired it, but not else.—She made me very little answer, but has since told me, she did not think it at that time.

I embarked at Tower-warf at four o'clock in the morning, and arrived at Amsterdam the next day by three o'clock in the afternoon. I had several letters of recommendation to my old master's friends, who received me very graciously. Indeed one of the chief ministers was particularly good to me; he kept me at his own house a long while, and took great pleasure in asking me questions, which I answered with delight, being always ready to say, "*Come unto me all ye that fear GOD and I will tell what he hath done for my soul.*" I cannot but admire the footsteps of Providence, astonished that I should be so wonderfully preserved! Though the grandson of a king, I have wanted bread, and should have been glad with the hardest crust I ever saw. I who at home, was surrounded and guarded by slaves, so that no indifferent person might approach me, and cloathed with gold, have been inhumanly threatened with death; and frequently wanted cloathing to defend me from the inclemency of the weather; yet I never murmured, nor was I ever discontented. I am willing, and even desirous to be counted as nothing, a stranger in the world, and a pilgrim here; for "*I know that my* REDEEMER *liveth*," and I am thankful for every trial and trouble that I have met with, as I am not without hope that they have been all sanctified to me.

The Calvinist ministers desired to hear my experience from myself, which proposal I was very well pleased with; so I stood before thirty-eight ministers every Thursday, for seven weeks together, and they were all very well satisfied, and persuaded I was what I pretended to be. They wrote down my experience as I spoke it: and the LORD ALMIGHTY was with me at that time in a remarkable manner, and gave me words and enabled me to answer them; so great was his mercy to take me in hand a poor blind heathen.

At this time a very rich merchant in AMSTERDAM, offered to take me into his family in the capacity of his butler, and I very willingly accepted it. He was a gracious worthy gentleman, and very good to me. He treated me more like a friend than a servant. I tarried there a twelve-month but was not thoroughly contented, I wanted to see my wife; (that is now) and for that reason I wished to return to ENGLAND, I wrote to her once in my absence, but she did not answer my letter; and I must acknowledge if she had, it would have given me a less opinion of her. My master and mistress persuaded me much not to leave them, and likewise their two sons who entertained a good opinion of me; and if I had found my Betty married on my arrival in ENGLAND, I should have returned to them again immediately.

My lady purposed my marrying her maid; she was an agreeable young woman, had saved a great deal of money, but I could not fancy her, though she was willing to accept of me, but I told her, my inclinations were engaged in ENGLAND, and I could think of no other person. On my return home, I found my Betty disengaged. She had refused several offers in my absence, and told her sister, that she thought if ever she married, I was to be her husband.

Soon after I came home, I waited on Doctor Gifford, who took me into his family, and was exceedingly good to me. The character of this pious worthy gentleman is well known, my praise can be of no use or signification at all. I hope I shall ever gratefully remember the many favours I have received from him. Soon after I came to Doctor Gifford, I expressed a desire to be admitted into their church, and sit down with them; they told me I must first be baptized; so I gave in my experience before the church, with which they were very well satisfied, and I was baptized by Dr. Gifford with some others.

I then made known my intention of being married; but I found there were many objections against it, because the person I had fixed on was poor. She was a widow, her husband had left her in debt, and with a child, so that they persuaded me against it out of real regard to me. But I had promised and was resolved to have her; as I knew her to be a gracious woman, her poverty was no objection to me, as they had nothing else to say against her. When my friends found they could not alter my opinion respecting her, they wrote to Mr. Allen, the minister she attended, to persuade her to leave me; but he replied he would not interfere at all, that we might do as we would. I was resolved all my wife's little debt should be paid before we were married; so that I sold almost every thing I had, with all the money I could raise, cleared all that she owed, and I never did any thing with a better will in all my life, because I firmly believed that we should be very happy together, and so it proved, for she was given me from the LORD. And I have found her a blessed partner, and we have never repented, though we have gone through many great troubles and difficulties.

My wife got a very good living at weaving, and could do extremely well; but just at that time there was great disturbance among the weavers: so that I was afraid to let my wife work, least they should insist on my being one of the rioters, which I could not think of, and, possibly, if I had refused to do so, they would have knocked me on the head. So that by these means my wife could get no employ, neither had I work enough to maintain my family. We had not yet been married a year before all these misfortunes overtook us.

Just at this time a gentleman, that seemed much concerned for us, advised us to go into Essex with him, and promised to get me employed. I accepted his kind proposal, and he spoke to a friend of his, a quaker, a gentleman of large fortune, who resided a little way out of the town of Colchester, his name was Handbarar; he ordered his steward to set me to work.

There were several employed in the same way with myself. I was very thankful and contented though my wages were but small. I was allowed but eight-pence a day and found myself; but after I had been in this situation for a fortnight, my master, being told that a black was at work for him, had an inclination to see me. He was pleased to talk with me for some time, and at last enquired what wages I had; when I told him, he declared it was too little, and immediately ordered his steward to let me have eighteen-pence a day, which he constantly gave me after; and I then did extremely well.

I did not bring my wife with me: I came first

alone, and it was my design, if things answered according to our wishes, to send for her—I was now thinking to desire her to come to me, when I received a letter to inform me that she was just brought to bed, and in want of many necessaries. This news was a great trial to me, and a fresh affliction: but my GOD, *faithful and abundant in mercy*, forsook me not in this trouble. As I could not read writing, I was obliged to apply to some person to read the letter I received, relative to my wife. I was directed by the good providence of GOD, to a worthy young gentleman, a quaker, and friend of my master's. I desired he would take the trouble to read my letter for me, which he readily complied with, and was greatly moved and affected at the contents; insomuch that he said he would undertake to make a gathering for me, which he did and was the first to contribute to it himself. The money was sent that evening to London by a person who happened to be going there; nor was this *all* the goodness I experienced from these kind friends, for as soon as my wife came about and was fit to travel, they sent for her to me, and were at the whole expence of her coming; so evidently has the love and mercy of GOD appeared through every trouble that ever I experienced. We went on very comfortably all the summer. We lived in a little cottage near Mr. Handbarar's house; but when the winter came on I was discharged, as he had no farther occasion for me. And now the prospect began to darken upon us again. We thought it most adviseable to move our habitation a little nearer to the town, as the house we lived in was very cold, and wet, and ready to tumble down.

The boundless goodness of GOD to me has been so very great, that with the most humble gratitude I desire to prostrate myself before him; for I have been wonderfully supported in every affliction—My GOD never left me, I perceived light *full* through the thickest darkness.

My dear wife and I were now both unemployed, we could get nothing to do; the winter proved remarkably severe, and we were reduced to the greatest distress imaginable. I was always very shy of asking for any thing, I could never beg, neither did I choose to make known our wants to any person, for fear of offending, as we were entire strangers; but our last bit of bread was gone, and I was obliged to think of something to do for our support. I did not mind for myself at all, but to see my dear wife and children in want, pierced me to the heart. I now blamed myself for bringing her from London, as doubtless had we continued there, we might have found friends to have kept us from starving. The snow was at this season remarkably deep, so that we could see no prospect of being relieved: In this melancholy situation, not knowing what step to pursue, I resolved to make my case known to a gentleman's gardener, that lived near us, and intreat him to employ me; but when I came to him my courage failed me, and I was ashamed to make known our real situation: I endeavoured all I could to prevail on him to set me to work, but to no purpose, he assured me it was not in his power; but just when I was about to leave him, he asked me if I would accept of some carrots? I took them with great thankfulness, and carried them home; he gave me four, they were very large and fine. We had nothing to make a fire with, so consequently could not boil them, but was glad to have them to eat *raw*. Our youngest child was then an infant, so that my wife was obliged to chew it, and fed her in that manner for several days. We allowed ourselves but one every day, least they should not last till we could get some other supply. I was unwilling to eat at all myself, nor would I take any the last day that we continued in this situation, as I could not bear the thought that my wife and children would be in want of the means of support. We lived in this manner, till our carrots were gone; then my wife began to lament because of our poor babies, but I comforted her all I could; still hoping and believing, that my GOD would not let us die, but that it would please him to relieve us, which he did almost by a miracle.

We went to bed as usual, before it was quite dark, (as we had neither fire nor candle) but had not been there long, before some person knocked at the door and enquired if *James Albert* lived there? I answered in the affirmative, and rose immediately; as soon as I opened the door, I found it was the servant of an eminent attorney who resided at *Colchester*. He asked me how it was with me? if I was not almost starved; I burst out a crying, and told him I was indeed. He said his master supposed so, and that he wanted to speak with me, and I must return with him. This gentleman's name was *Danniel*, he was a sincere good Christian. He used to stand and talk with me frequently, when I worked on the road for Mr. *Handbarar*, and would have employed me himself, if I had wanted work: When I came to his house, he told me that he had thought a great deal about me of late, and was apprehensive that I must be in want, and could not be satisfied till he had sent to enquire after me. I made known my distress to him, at which he was greatly affected, and generously gave me a guinea, and promised to be kind to me in future. I could not help exclaiming, *Oh! the boundless mercies of my* GOD! I prayed unto him and he has heard me; I trusted in him and he has preserved me;

where shall I begin to praise him, or how shall I love him enough?

I went immediately and bought some bread and cheese, and coal, and carried them home. My dear wife was rejoiced to see me return with something to eat. She instantly got up and dressed our babies, while I made a fire, and the first nobility in the land never made a better meal. We did not forget to thank the LORD for all his goodness to us. Soon after this, as the spring came on, Mr. Peter Danniel employed me in helping to pull down a house, and rebuilding it. I had then very good work, and full employ; he sent for my wife and children to Colchester, and provided us a house where we lived very comfortably: I hope I shall always gratefully acknowledge his kindness to myself and family. I worked at this house for more than a year, till it was finished, and after that I was employed by several successively, and was never so happy as when I had something to do; but perceiving the winter coming on, and work rather slack, I was apprehensive that we should again be in want, or become troublesome to our friends.

I had at this time an offer made me of going to Norwich, and having constant employ. My wife seemed pleased with this proposal, as she supposed she might get work there in the weaving manufactory, being the business she was brought up to, and more likely to succeed there than in any other place; and we thought as we had an opportunity of moving to a town where we might both be employed, it was most advisable to do so; and that probably we might settle there for our lives. When this step was resolved on, I went first alone to see how it would answer, which I very much repented after, for it was not in my power immediately to send my wife any supply, as I fell into the hands of a master that was neither kind nor considerate, and she was reduced to great distress, so that she was obliged to sell the few goods that we had, and when I sent for her, she was under the disagreeable necessity of parting with our bed.

When she came to Norwich, I hired a room ready furnished. I experienced a great deal of difference in the carriage of my master from what I had been accustomed to from some of my other masters; he was very irregular in his payments to me: My wife hired a loom, and wove all the leisure time she had, and we began to do very well, till we were overtaken by fresh misfortunes. Our three poor children fell ill of the small-pox, this was a great trial to us, but still I was persuaded in myself we should not be forsaken. I did all in my power to keep my dear partner's spirits from sinking; as her whole attention was now taken up with the children, she could mind nothing else, and all I could get was but little to support a family in such a situation, besides paying for the hire of our room, which I was obliged to omit doing for several weeks; but the woman to whom we were indebted would not excuse us, though I promised she should have the first money we could get after my children came about, but she would not be satisfied, and had the cruelty to threaten us, that if we did not pay her immediately, she would turn us all into the street.

The apprehension of this, plunged me into the deepest distress, considering the situation of my poor babies, if they had been in health, I should have been less sensible of this misfortune. But my GOD *still faithful to his promise,* raised me a friend, Mr. Henry Gurdney, a quaker, a gracious gentleman heard of our distress, he sent a servant of his own to the woman we hired our room of, paid our rent, and bought all the goods, with my wife's loom, and gave it us all.

Some other gentlemen hearing of his design; were pleased to assist him in these generous acts; for which we never can be thankful enough; after this my children soon came about, and we began to do pretty well again; my dear wife worked hard and constant when she could get work, but it was upon a disagreeable footing, her employ was so uncertain, sometimes she could get nothing to do, and at other times when the weavers of Norwich had orders from

London, they were so excessively hurried, that the people they employed were obliged to work on the *Sabbathday*, but this my wife would never do; and it was matter of uneasiness to us that we could not get our living in a regular manner, though we were both diligent, industrious, and willing to work. I was far from being happy in my master, he did not use me well, I could scarcely ever get my money from him; but I continued patient, till it pleased GOD to alter my situation.

My worthy friend Mr. Gurdney, advised me to follow the employment of chopping chaff, and bought me an instrument for that purpose. There were but few people in the town that made this their business besides myself, so that I did very well indeed, and became quite easy and happy. But we did not continue long in this comfortable state, many of the inferior people were envious and ill-natured, and set up the same employ and worked under price on purpose to get my business from me, and they succeeded so well that I could hardly get any thing to do, and became again unfortunate: Nor did this misfortune come alone, for just at this time we lost one of our little girls who died of a fever: This circumstance occasioned us new troubles, for the baptist minister refused to bury her because we were not their members; the parson of the parish denied because she had never been baptized: I applied to the quakers, but met with no success; this was one of the greatest trials I had ever met with, as we did not know what to do with our poor baby: At length I resolved to dig a grave in the garden behind the house, and bury her there; when the parson of the parish sent for to tell me he would bury the child, but did not choose to read the burial service over her. I told him I did not care whether he would or no, as the child could not hear it.

We met with a great deal of ill treatment after this, and found it very difficult to live: We could scarcely get work to do, and were obliged to pawn our cloaths, we were ready to sink under our troubles; when I proposed to my wife to go to Kidderminster, and try if we could do there—I had always an inclination for that place, and now more than ever, as I had heard Mr Fawcet mentioned in the most respectful manner, as a pious worthy gentleman, and I had seen his name in a favourite book of mine, called Baxter's *Saints Everlasting Rest*; and as the manufactory at Kidderminster seemed to promise my wife some employment, she readily came into my way of thinking.

I left her once more, and set out for Kidderminster, in order to judge if the situation would suit us. As soon as I came there I waited immediately on

Mr. Fawcet, who was pleased to receive me very kindly, and recommended me to Mr. Watson, who employed me in twisting silk and worsted together. I continued here about a fortnight, and when I thought it would answer our expectation, I returned to Norwich, to fetch my wife; she was then near her time, and too much indisposed, so we were obliged to tarry until she was brought to bed, and as soon as she could conveniently travel, we came to Kidderminster, but we brought nothing with us, as we were obliged to sell all we had to pay our debts, and the expences of my wife's illness, &c.

Such is our situation at present—My wife, by hard labour at the loom, does every thing that can be expected from her towards the maintenance of our family; and GOD is pleased to incline the hearts of his people at times to yield us their charitable assistance, being myself through age and infirmity able to contribute but little to their support. As pilgrims, and very poor pilgrims, we are travelling through many difficulties towards our HEAVENLY HOME, and waiting patiently for his gracious call, when the LORD shall deliver us out of the evils of this present world, and bring us to the EVERLASTING GLORIES of the world to come.——TO HIM be PRAISE for EVER and EVER. AMEN.

Published 1772

IGNATIUS SANCHO

Sancho (1729–1780) was the first African play-wright, theatre critic, art critic, composer and patron of the arts in Britain. He was born on a slave ship crossing the Atlantic Ocean and orphaned in infancy. He was later educated and employed by the Duke of Montagu, and on his retirement in 1773 Sancho opened a grocery shop. In 1768, the duke employed the artist Thomas Gainsborough to paint Sancho's portrait. The portrait has brought Sancho some fame, but he was also a bibliophile, composer and writer, although his two plays and a book entitled *Theory of Music* have not survived. During his lifetime he was chiefly known for his letter writing, which commenced during 1766. Sancho wrote to eminent acquaintances and friends on a variety of subjects including slavery, colonialism and everyday London life. The following extracts focus mainly on his horror regarding the Gordon Riots in London in June 1780.

Letters of the Late Ignatius Sancho

To Mr. R——.

October 20, 1779.

Zounds, Sir! would you believe—Ireland has the * * * to claim the advantages of a free unlimited trade—or they will join in the American dance!— What a pack of * * * are * * *! I think the wisest thing administration can do (and I dare wager they will) is to stop the exportation of potatoes—and repeal the act for the encouragement of growing tobacco * * *. It is reported here (from excellent authority) that the people at large surrounded the Irish parliament, and made the members—the courtiers—the formists and non-cons—cats—culls— and pimpwhiskins—all—all subscribe to their—. Well, but what says your brother—no better news I much fear from that quarter.—Oh, this poor ruined country!—ruined by its success—and the choicest blessings the Great Father of Heaven could shower down upon us—ruined by victories—arts—arms— and unbounded commerce—for pride accompanied those blessings—and like a cankerworm has eaten into the heart of our political body.—The Dutch have given up the Serapis and the Scarborough, and detained Paul Jones twenty-four hours after their failing:—how they will balance accounts with France, I know not; but I do believe the Mynheers will get into a scrape.

Tell Mr. B——the Pyefleets fluctuate in price like the stocks, and were done this morning at Billingsgate change, at I*l*. 6*s*. 8*d*. *per* bushel; but I have sent them this evening properly directed—also a book of *Cogniscenti dilitanti divertimenti*.—As for the ladies, I cannot say anything in justice to their merits or my own feelings:—therefore I am silent—write soon—a decent, plain, and intelligible letter—a letter that a body may read with pleasure and improvement—none of your circumroundabouts for

    I. SANCHO.

LETTER CXXXIII.

To J——s——, ESQ.

Charles-Street, June 6, 1780.

Dear and most respected sir,

In the midst of the most cruel and ridiculous confusion—I am now set down to give you a very imperfect sketch of the maddest people—that the maddest times were ever plagued with.—The public prints have informed you (without doubt) of last Friday's transactions;—the insanity of Ld. G. G. and the worse than Negro barbarity of the populace; the burnings and devastations of each night—you will also see in the prints;—this day, by consent, was set apart for the farther consideration of the wished for repeal;—the people (who had their proper cue from his lordship) assembled by ten o'clock in the morning.—Lord N——h, who had been up in council at home till four in the morning, got to the house before eleven, just a quarter of an hour before the associators reached Palace-yard:—but, I should tell you, in council there was a deputation from all parties;—the S——party were for prosecuting Lord G——, and leaving him at large;—the At—y G—— I laughed at the idea, and declared it was doing just nothing;—the M——y were for his expulsion, and so dropping him gently into insignificancy;—that was thought wrong, as he would still be industrious in mischief;—the R——m party, I should suppose, you will think counselled best, which is, this day to expel him the house—commit him to the Tower— and then prosecute him at leisure—by which means he will lose the opportunity of getting a seat in the next parliament—and have decent leisure to repent him of the heavy evils he has occasioned.—There is at this present moment at least a hundred thousand poor, miserable ragged rabble, from twelve to sixty years of age, with blue cockades in their hats— besides half as many women and children—all parading the streets—the bridge—the park—ready for any and every mischief.—Gracious God! what's the matter now? I was obliged to leave off—the shouts of the mob—the horrid clashing of swords— and the clutter of a multitude in swiftest motion—drew me to the door—when every one in the street was employed in shutting up shop—It is now just five o' clock—the ballad-singers are exhausting their musical talents with the downfall of Popery, S—h, and N—h. Lord S—h narrowly escaped with life about an hour since;—the mob seized his chariot going to the house, broke his glasses, and, in struggling to get his lordship out, somehow have cut his face; the guards flew to his assistanec—the light-horse scowered the road, got his chariot, escorted him from the coffee-house, where he had fled for protection, to his carriage, and guarded him bleeding very fast home. This—this—is liberty! genuine British liberty!— This instant about two thousand liberty boys are swearing and swaggering by with large sticks—thus armed in hopes of meeting with the Irish chairmen and labourers—all the guards are out—and all the horse;—the poor fellows are just worn out for want of rest—having been on duty ever since Friday. Thank heaven, it rains; may it increase, so as to send these deluded wretches safe to their homes, their families, and wives! About two this afternoon a large party took it into their heads to visit the King and Queen, and entered the Park for that purpose—but found the guard too numerous to be forced, and after some useless attempts gave it up. It is reported, the house will either be prorogued, or parliament dissolved, this evening—as it is in vain to think of attending any business while this anarchy lasts.

I cannot but felicitate you, my good friend, upon the happy distance you are placed from our scene of confusion.—May soul Discord and her cursed train never nearer approach your blessed abode! Tell Mrs. S——, her good heart would ach, did she see the anxiety, the woe, in the faces of mothers, wives, and sweethearts, each equally anxious for the object of their wishes, the beloved of their hearts. Mrs. Sancho and self both cordially join in love and gratitude, and every good wish—crowned with the peace of God, which passeth all understanding, &c.

I am, dear Sir,

 Yours ever by inclination,

 IGN. SANCHO.

Postscript,

The Sardinian ambassador offered 500 guineas to the rabble, to save a painting of our Saviour from the flames, and 1000 guineas not to destroy an exceeding fine organ: the gentry told him, they would burn him if they could get at him, and destroyed the picture and organ directly. I am not sorry I was born in Africa.—I shall tire you, I fear—and, if I cannot get a frank, make you pay dear for bad news. There is about a thousand mad men, armed with clubs, bludgeons, and crows, just now set off for Newgate, to liberate, they say, their honest comrades.—I wish they do not some of them lose their lives of liberty before morning. It is thought by many who discern deeply, that there is more at the bottom of this business than merely the repeal of an act—which as has yet produced no bad consequences, and perhaps never might.—I am forced to own, that I am for an universal toleration. Let us convert by our example, and conquer by our meekness and brotherly love!

Eight o'clock. Lord G——G——has this moment announced to my Lords the mob—that the act shall be repealed this evening:—upon this, they gave a hundred chears—took the horses from his hackney-coach, and rolled him full jollily away:—they are huzzaing now ready to crack their throats.

Huzza!

I am forced to conclude for want of room—the remainder in our next.

LETTER CXXXIV.

To J——s——, ESQ.

Charles Street, June 9, 1780.

My dear sir,

Government is sunk in lethargic stupor—anarchy reigns—when I look back to the glorious time of a George II. and a Pitt's administration—my heart sinks at the bitter contrast. We may now say of England, as was heretofore said of Great Babylon—"the beauty of the excellency of "the Chaldees is no more;"—the Fleet Prison, the Marshalsea, King's-Bench, both Compters, Clerkenwell, and Tothill-Fields, with Newgate, are slung open;—Newgate partly burned, and 300 felons, from thence only, let loose upon the world. Lord M——'s house in town suffered martyrdom; and his sweet box at Caen Wood escaped almost miraculously, for the mob had just arrived, and were beginning with it, when a strong detachment from the guards and light-horse came most critically to its rescue—the library, and, what is of more consequence, papers and deeds of vast value, were all cruelly consumed in the flames. Ld. N—'s house was attacked; but they had previous notice, and were ready for them. The Bank, the Treasury, and thirty of the chief noblemen's houses, are doomed to suffer by the insurgents. There were six of the rioters killed at Ld. M——'s, and, what is remarkable, a daring chap, escaped from Newgate, condemned to die this day, was the most active in mischief at Ld. M——'s, and was the first person shot by the soldiers; so he found death a few hours sooner than if he had not been released.—The ministry have tried lenity, and have experienced its inutility; and martial law is this night to be declared.—If any body of people above ten in number are seen together, and refuse to disperse, they are to be fired at without any further ceremony—so we expect terrible work before morning.—The insurgents visited the Tower, but it would not do:—they had better luck in the Artillery-ground, where they found and took to their use 500 stand of arms; a great error in city politics, not to have secured them first.—It is wonderful to hear the execrable nonsense that is industriously circulated amongst the credulous mob, who are told his M——y regularly goes to mass at Ld. P—re's chaple—and they believe it, and that he pays out of his privy purse Peter-pence to Rome. Such is the temper of the times—from too relaxed a government;—and a King and Queen on the throne who possess every virtue. May God, in his mercy, grant that the present scourge may operate to our repentance and amendment! that it may produce the fruits of better thinking, better doing, and in the end make us a wise, virtuous, and happy people!—I am, dear Sir, truly, Mrs. S——'s and your most grateful and obliged friend and servant,

I. SANCHO.

The remainder in our next.

Half past nine o'clock,

King's-Bench prison is now in flames, and the prisoners at large; two fires in Holborn now burning.

LETTER CXXXV.

To J——S——, Esq.

June 9, 1780.

Dear sir,

Happily for us, the tumult begins to subside:— last night much was threatened, but nothing done—except in the early part of the evening, when about fourscore or an hundred of the reformers got decently knocked on the head;—they were half killed by Mr. Langdale's spirits—so fell an easy conquest to the bayonet and butt-end.—There are about fifty taken prisoners—and not a blue cockade to be seen:—the streets once more wear the face of peace—and men seem once more to resume their accustomed employments.—

The greatest losses have fallen upon the great distiller near Holborn-bridge, and Lord M——; the former, alas! has lost his whole fortune;—the latter, the greatest and best collection of manuscript writings, with one of the finest libraries in the kingdom. Shall we call it a judgement?—or what shall we call it? The thunder of their vengeance has fallen upon Gin and Law—the two most inflammatory things in the Christian world.—We have a Coxheath and Warley of our own; Hyde Park has a grand encampment, with artillery, Park, &c. &c. St. James's Park has ditto—upon a smaller scale. The Parks, and our West end of the town, exhibit the features of French government. This minute, thank God! this moment Lord G. G. is taken. Sir F. Molineux has him safe at the horse-guards. Bravo! he is, now going in state in an old hackney-coach, escorted by a regiment of militia and troop of light horse, to his apartments in the Tower.

"Off with his head—so much—for Buckingham."

We have taken this day numbers of the poor wretches, in so much we know not where to place them. Blessed be the Lord! we trust this affair is pretty well concluded.—If any thing transpires worth your notice—you shall hear from

Your much obliged, &c. &c.

IGN. SANCHO.

Best regards attend Mrs. S——. His lordship was taken at five o'clock this evening—betts run fifteen to five, Lord G—G—is hanged in eight days:—he wished much to speak to his Majesty on Wednesday, but was of course refused.

Published 1782

Olaudah Equiano

Olaudah Equiano (*c.*1745–1797) was born in the kingdom of Benin, now in south-eastern Nigeria. When he was about eleven, Equiano and his sister were kidnapped by other Africans. Equiano was sold to Europeans who transported him to the Americas where he was sold and renamed Gustavus Vassa. Equiano managed to buy his own freedom in 1766. He then worked as a mariner and hairdresser and converted to Methodism. He began his abolitionist activities in the 1770s, writing regularly in the press. In the 1780s he worked with other African abolitionists, the Sons of Africa, as well as radicals in Britain and Ireland. His famous *Narrative* of 1789 became a bestseller and appeared in many editions and translations. Equiano lectured throughout the British Isles, giving a first-hand account of life in Africa and his own experience of human trafficking and slavery. In this extract, Equiano describes some of his early experiences of Britain.

The Interesting Narrative of the Life of Olaudah Equiano, or Gustavus Vassa, the African

It was about the beginning of the spring, 1757, when I arrived in *England*, and I was near twelve years of age at that time. I was very much struck with the buildings and the pavement of the streets in *Falmouth*; and, indeed, every object I saw filled me with fresh surprise. One morning, when I got upon deck, I perceived it covered all over with the snow that fell over-night: as I had never seen any thing of the kind before, I thought it was salt; so I immediately ran down to the mate and desired him, as well as I could, to come and see how somebody in the night had thrown salt all over the deck. He, knowing what it was, desired me to bring some of it down to him: accordingly I took up a handful of it, which I found very cold indeed; and when I brought it to him he desired me to taste it. I did so, and was surprised above measure. I then asked him what it was; he told me it was snow; but I could not by any means understand him. He asked me if we had no such thing in my country; and I told him, No. I then asked him the use of it, and who made it: he told me a great man in the heavens, called God: but here again I was to all intents and purposes, at a loss to understand him; and the more so, when, a little after, I saw the air filled with it, in a heavy shower, which fell down on the same day. After this I went to church; and having never been at such a place before, I was amazed at seeing and hearing the service; I asked all I could about it; and they gave me to understand it was *worshipping God, who made us and all things*. I was still at a loss, and got into an endless field of enquiries, as well as I was able to speak and ask about things. However, my dear little friend *Dick* used to be my best interpreter; for I could make free with him, and he always instructed me with pleasure: and from what I could understand by him of this God, and in seeing that these white people did not sell one another as we did, I was much pleased; and in this I thought they were much happier than we *Africans*. I was astonished at the wisdom of the white people in all things I beheld; but greatly amazed at their not sacrificing, or making any offerings, and *eating with unwashed hands, and touching the dead*. I also could not help remarking the particular slenderness of their women, which I did not at first like, and I thought them not so modest and shamefaced as the *African* women.

[. . .]

In pursuance of our orders we sailed from *Portsmouth* for the *Thames*, and arrived at *Deptford* the

10th of *December*, where we cast anchor just as it was high water. The ship was up about half an hour, when my master ordered the barge to be manned: and all in an instant, without having before given me the least reason to suspect any thing of the matter, he forced me into the barge, saying, I was going to leave him, but he would take care I did not. I was so struck with the unexpectedness of this proceeding, that for some time I did not make a reply; only I made an offer to go for my books and chest of clothes, but he swore I should not move out of his sight; and if I did he would cut my throat, at the same time taking out his hanger. I began, however, to collect myself; and plucking up courage, I told him that I was free, and he could not by law serve me so. But this only enraged him the more; and he continued to swear, and said he would soon let me know whether he would or not, and at that instant sprung himself into the barge, to the astonishment and sorrow of all on board. The tide, rather unluckily for me, had just turned downward, so that we quickly fell down the river along with it, till we came among some outward-bound *West-India-men*; for he was resolved to put me on board the first vessel he could get to receive me. The boat's crew, who pulled against their will, became quite faint at different times, and would have gone ashore, but he would not let them. Some of them strove then to cheer me, and told me he could not sell me, and that they would stand by me, which revived me a little, and I still entertained hopes; for as they pulled along he asked some vessels to receive me, and they refused. But, just as we had got a little below *Gravesend*, we came alongside of a ship going away the next tide for the *West-Indies*; her name was the *Charming Sally*, Captain *James Doran*; and my master went on board and agreed with him for me: and in a little time I was sent for into the cabin. When I came there Captain *Doran* asked me if I knew him: I answered I did not;—"Then," said he, "You are now my slave." I told him my master could not sell me to him, nor to any one else. "Why," said he, "Did not your master buy you?" I confessed he did. "But I have served him," said I, "many years, and he has taken all my wages and prize-money, for I had only got one six-pence during the war; besides this I have been baptized; and, by the laws of the land, no man has a right to sell me:" and I added, that I had heard a lawyer, and others, at different times, tell my master so. They both then said, that those people who told me so, were not my friends: but I replied—"It was very extraordinary that other people did not know the law as well as they." Upon this Captain *Doran* said I talked too much *English*, and if I did not behave myself well, and be quiet, he had a method on board to make me. I was too well convinced of his power over me to doubt what he said; and my former sufferings in the slave-ship presenting themseves to my mind, the recollection of them made me shudder. However, before I retired I told them, that as I could not get any right among men here, I hoped I should hereafter in Heaven, and I immediately left the cabin, filled with resentment and sorrow. The only coat I had with me my master took away with him, and said, "If your prize-money had been £10,000, I had a right to it all, and would have taken it." I had about nine guineas, which, during my long sea-faring life, I had scraped together from trifling perquisites and little ventures; and I hid it that instant, least my master should take that from me likewise, still hoping that, by some means or other, I should make my escape to the shore; and indeed some of my old shipmates told me not to despair, for they would get me back again; and that, as soon as they could get their pay, they would immediately come to *Portsmouth* to me, where this ship was going: but, alas! all my hopes were baffled, and the hour of my deliverance was as yet far off. My master, having soon concluded his bargain with the captain, came out of the cabin, and he and his people got into the boat and put off; I followed them with aching eyes as long as I could, and when they were out of sight I threw myself on the deck with a heart ready to burst with sorrow and anguish.

[. . .]

We had a most prosperous voyage, and, at the end of seven weeks, arrived at *Cherry Garden* stairs. Thus were my longing eyes once more gratified with a sight of *London*, after having been absent from it above four years. I immediately received my wages, and I never earned seven guineas so quick before; I had thirty-seven guineas in all, when I got cleared of the ship. I now entered upon a scene quite new to me, but full of hope. In this situation, my first thoughts were to look out for some of my former friends, and amongst the first of those were the Miss *Guerins*. As soon as I had regaled myself, I went in quest of those kind ladies, whom I was very impatient to see, and, with some difficulty and perseverance, I found them at *May's-hill, Greenwich*. They were most agreeably surprised to see me, and I quite overjoyed at meeting with them. I told them my history, at which they expressed great wonder, and freely acknowledged it did their cousin, Captain *Pascal*, no honour. He then visited there frequently; and I met him, four or five days after, in *Greenwich* park. When he saw me, he appeared a good deal surprised, and asked me how I came back? I answered, 'In a ship.' To which he replied drily, 'I suppose you did not walk back to *London* on water.' As I saw, by his manner, that he did not seem to be sorry for his behaviour to me, and that I had not much reason to expect any favour from him, I told him, that he had used me very ill, after I had been such a faithful servant to him for so many years; on which, without saying any more, he turned about, and went away. A few days after this, I met Captain *Pascal*, at Miss *Guerins'* house, and asked him for my prize-money. He said there was none due to me, for, if my prize-money had been 10,000 *l.* he had a right to it all. I told him, I was informed otherwise: on which, he bade me defiance; and in a bantering tone, desired me to commence a law-suit against him for it, 'There are lawyers enough,' said he, 'that will take the cause in hand, and you had better try it.' I told him then, that I would try it, which enraged him very much; however, out of regard to the ladies, I remained still, and never made any farther demand of my right.

Some time afterwards, these friendly ladies asked me, what I meant to do with myself, and how they could assist me. I thanked them, and said, if they pleased I would be their servant; but if not, I had thirty-seven guineas, which would support me for some time, and I would be much obliged to them to

41

recommend me to some person who would teach me a trade whereby I might earn my living. They answered me very politely, that they were sorry it did not suit them to take me as their servant, and asked me what business I should like to learn? I said, hair-dressing. They then promised to asssist me in this: and soon after, they recommended me to a gentle-man whom I had known before, one Captain *O'Hara*, who treated me with much kindness, and procured me a master, a hair-dresser, in *Coventry Court, Haymarket*, with whom he placed me. I was with this man from September, till the February following. In that time we had a neighbour in the same *Court*, who taught the French-horn. He used to blow it so well, that I was charmed with it, and agreed with him to teach me to blow it. Accordingly he took me in hand, and began to instruct me, and I soon learned all the three parts. I took great delight in blowing on this instrument, the evenings being long; and, besides, that I was fond of it, I did not like to be idle, and it filled up my vacant hours innocently. At this time, also, I agreed with the Rev. Mr. *Greg-ory*, who lived in the same court, where he kept an academy and an evening school, to improve me in arithmetic. This he did as far as Barter and Alliga-tion; so that all the time I was here I was entirely employed. In February, 1768, I hired myself to

Dr. *Charles Irving*, in *Pall-mall*, so celebrated for his successful experiments in making sea-water fresh; and here I had plenty of hair-dressing to improve my hand. This gentleman was an excellent master; he was exceedingly kind and good-tempered; and allowed me in the evenings to attend my schools, which I esteemed a great blessing; therefore I thanked God and him for it, and used all diligence to improve the opportunity. This diligence and attention recommended me to the notice and care of my three preceptors, who, on their parts, bestowed a great deal of pains in my instruction, and besides were all very kind to me. My wages, however, which were by two thirds less than ever I had in my life (for I had only 12 *l.* per annum) I soon found would not be sufficient to defray this extraordinary expence of masters, and my own necessary expences; my old thirty-seven guineas had by this time worn away all to one. I thought it best, therefore, to try the sea again, in quest of more money, as I had been bred to it, and had hitherto found the profession of it successful.—I had also a very great desire to see *Turkey*, and I now determined to gratify it. Accordingly, in the month of May, 1768, I told the doctor my wish to go to sea again, to which he made no opposition; and we parted on friendly terms.—

Published 1789

Ottobah Cugoano

Ottobah Cugoano (*c.*1757–*c.*1791) was born around 1757 in a coastal village in what is today Ghana. He was kidnapped as a teenager by African traffickers who sold him to Europeans. Initially transported to Grenada, in 1772 he was taken to England, where he educated himself and was also sent to school by his owner. Subsequently he was employed as a servant for the painters Richard and Maria Cosway and began to work with other African abolitionists and Granville Sharpe in London. In 1787, possibly with Equiano's assistance, he published his major work. In 1791 Cugoano published a shorter version addressed to the Sons of Africa, but nothing is known of him after this date. In the following extracts he condemns the massacre on the slave ship *Zong*, the human traffickers and Britain's parliament, and is critical of attempts to repatriate impoverished Africans from Britain to Sierra Leone.

Thoughts and Sentiments on the Evil and Wicked Traffic of the Slavery and Commerce of the Human Species

But whereas the people of Great-Britain having now acquired a greater share in that iniquitous commerce than all the rest together, they are the first that ought to set an example, lest they have to repent for their wickedness when it becomes too late; lest some impending calamity should speedily burst forth against them, and lest a just retribution for their enormous crimes, and a continuance in committing similar deeds of barbarity and injustice should involve them in ruin. For we may be assured that God will certainly avenge himself of such heinous transgressors of his law, and of all those planters and merchants, and of all others, who are the authors of the Africans graves, severities, and cruel punishments, and no plea of any absolute necessity can possibly excuse them. And as the inhabitants of Great-Britain, and the inhabitants of the colonies, seem almost equally guilty of the oppression, there is great reason for both to dread the severe vengeance of Almighty God upon them, and upon all such notorious workers of wickedness; for it is evident that the legislature of Great-Britain patronises and encourages them, and shares in the infamous profits of the slavery of the Africans. It is therefore necessary that the inhabitants of the British nation should seriously consider these things for their own good and safety, as well as for our benefit and deliverance, and that they may be sensible of their own error and danger, lest they provoke the vengeance of the Almighty against them. For what wickedness was there ever risen up so monstrous, and more likely to bring a heavy rod of destruction upon a nation, than the deeds committed by the West-Indian slavery, and the African slave trade. And even in that part of it carried on by the Liverpool and Bristol merchants, the many shocking and inhuman instances of their barbarity and cruelty are such, that every one that heareth thereof has reason to tremble, and cry out, *Should not the land tremble for this, and every one mourn that dwelleth therein*?

The vast carnage and murders committed by the British instigators of slavery, is attended with a very shocking, peculiar, and almost unheard of conception, according to the notion of the perpetrators of it; they either consider them as their own property, that they may do with as they please, in life or death; or that the taking away the life of a black man is of no more account than taking away the life of a beast. A very melancholy instance of this happened about the year 1780, as recorded in the courts of law; a master of a vessel bound to the Western Colonies, selected 132 of the most sickly of the black slaves, and ordered them to be thrown overboard into the sea, in order to recover their value from the insurers, as he had perceived that he was too late to get a good market for them in the West-Indies. On the trial, by the counsel for the owners of the vessel against the underwriters, their argument was, that the slaves were to be considered the same as horses; and their plea for throwing them into the sea, was nothing better than that it might be more necessary to throw them overboard to lighten their vessel than goods of greater value, or something to that effect. These poor creatures, it seems, were tied two and two together when they were thrown into the sea, left some of them might swim a little for the last gasp of air, and, with the animation of their approaching exit, breath their souls away to the gracious Father of spirits. Some of the last parcel, when they saw the fate of their companions, made their escape from tying by jumping overboard, and one was saved by means of a rope from some in the ship. The owners of the vessel, I suppose, (inhuman connivers of robbery, slavery, murder and fraud) were rather a little defeated in this, by bringing their villainy to light in a court of law; but the inhuman monster of a captain was kept out of the way of justice from getting hold of him. Though such perpetrators of murder and fraud should have been sought after from the British Dan in the East-Indies, to her Beershebah in the West.

[. . .]

Particular thanks is due to every one of that humane society of worthy and respectful gentlemen, whose liberality hath supported many of the Black poor about London. *Those that honor their Maker have mercy on the poor; and many blessings are upon the head of the just: may the fear of the Lord prolong their days, and cause their memory to be blessed, and may their number be encreased to fill their expectation with gladness*; for they have not only commiserated the poor in general, *but even those which are accounted as beasts, and imputed as vile in the sight of others*. The part that the British government has taken, to cooperate with them, has certainly a flattering and laudable appearance of doing some good; and the fitting out ships to supply a company of Black People with clothes and provisions, and to carry them to settle at Sierra Leona, in the West coast of Africa, as a free colony to Great-Britain, in a peaceable alliance with the inhabitants, has every appearance of honour, and the approbation of friends. According to the plan, humanity hath made its appearance in a more honorable way of colonization, than any Christian nation have ever done before, and may be productive of much good, if they continue to encourage and support them. But after all, there is some doubt whether their own flattering expectation in the manner as set forth to them, and the hope of their friends may not be defeated and rendered abortive; and there is some reason to fear, that they never will be settled as intended, in any permanent and peaceable way at Sierra Leona.

This prospect of settling a free colony to Great-Britain in a peaceable alliance with the inhabitants of Africa at Sierra Leona, has neither altogether met with the credulous approbation of the Africans here, nor yet been sought after with any prudent and right plan by the promoters of it. Had a treaty of agreement been first made with the inhabitants of Africa, and the terms and nature of such a settlement fixed upon, and its situation and boundary pointed out; then might the Africans, and others here, have embarked with a good prospect of enjoying happiness and prosperity themselves, and have gone with a hope of being able to render their services, in return, of some advantage to their friends and benefactors of Great-Britain. But as this was not done, and as they were to be hurried away at all events, come of them after what would; and yet, after all, to be delayed in the ships before they were set out from the coast, until many of them have perished with cold, and other disorders, and several of the most intelligent among them are dead, and others that, in all probability, would have been most useful for them were hindered from going, by means of some disagreeable jealousy of those who were appointed as governors, the great prospect of doing good seems all to be blown away. And so it appeared to some of those who are now gone, and at last, hap hazard, were obliged to go; who endeavoured in vain to get away by plunging into the water, that they might, if possible wade ashore, as dreading the prospect of their wretched fate, and as beholding their perilous situation, having every prospect of difficulty and surrounding danger.

What with the death of some of the original promoters and proposers of this charitable undertaking, and the death and deprivation of others that were to share the benefit of it, and by the adverse motives of those employed to be the conductors thereof, we think it will be more than what can be well expected, if we ever hear of any good in proportion to so great, well-designed, laudable and expensive charity. Many more of the Black People still in this country would have, with great gladness, embraced the opportunity, longing to reach their native land; but as the old saying is, A burnt child dreads the fire, some of these unfortunate sons and daughters of Africa have been severally unlawfully dragged away from their native abodes, under various pretences, by the insidious treachery of others, and have been brought into the hands of barbarous robbers and pirates, and, like sheep to the market, have been sold into captivity and slavery, and thereby have been deprived of their natural liberty and property, and every connection that they held dear and valuable, and subjected to the cruel service of the hard-hearted brutes called planters. But some of them, by various services either to the public or to individuals, as more particularly in the course of last war, have gotten their liberty again in this free country. They are thankful for the respite, but afraid of being ensnared again; for the European seafaring people in general, who trade to foreign parts, have such a prejudice against Black People, that they use them more like asses than men, so that a Black Man is scarcely ever safe among them. Much assiduity was made use to perswade the Black People in general to embrace the opportunity of going with this company of transports; but the wiser sort declined from all thoughts of it, unless they could hear of some better plan taking place for their security and safety. For as it seemed prudent and obvious to many of them taking heed to that sacred enquiry, *Doth a fountain send forth at the same place sweet water and bitter?* They were afraid that their doom would be to drink of the bitter water. For can it be readily conceived that government would establish a free colony for them nearly on the spot, while it supports its forts and garrisons, to ensnare, merchandize, and to carry others into captivity and slavery.

Published 1787

BOSTON KING

Boston King (*c.* 1760–*c.* 1802) was born on a South Carolina plantation to enslaved parents. He ran away from the plantation in 1780, joined the British Army and fought against the American colonists. As a Black Loyalist he was guaranteed freedom by the British, and in 1783 was evacuated to Nova Scotia with his wife. In 1791 the Black Loyalists were invited by the British government to migrate to Sierra Leone where they were promised their own land. Over a thousand accepted the offer, including Boston King, who wished to go as a missionary. He reached Africa in 1792 but his wife died soon after their arrival. He subsequently worked as a teacher and missionary before being offered the opportunity of an education in England. Arriving in 1794, he attended a school near Bristol, and it was there that he wrote his memoirs; here are some of his experiences in Britain.

Memoirs of the Life of Boston King,
A Black Preacher

In the year 1793, the gentlemen belonging to the Company told me, that if I would consent to go to England with the Governor, he would procure me two or three years schooling, that I might be better qualified to teach the natives. When this proposal was first mentioned to me, it seemed like an idle tale; but upon further conversation on the subject, difficulties were removed, and I consented. On the 26th of March 1794, we embarked for England, and arrived at Plymouth, after a pleasant voyage, on the 16th of May. On the 1st of June we got to the Thames, and soon after, Mrs. Paul, whom I was acquainted with in America, came to Wapping, and invited me to the New Chapel in the City-Road, where I was kindly received.

When I first arrived in England, I considered my great ignorance and inability, and that I was among a wise and judicious people, who were greatly my superiors in knowledge and understanding; these reflections had such an effect upon me, that I formed a resolution never to attempt to preach while I stayed in the country; but the kind importunity of the Preachers and others removed my objections, and I found it profitable to my own soul to be exercised in inviting sinners to Christ; particularly on Sunday, while I was preaching at Snowsfields-Chapel, the Lord blessed me abundantly, and I found a more cordial love to the White People than I had ever experienced before. In the former part of my life I had suffered greatly from the cruelty and injustice of the Whites, which induced me to look upon them, in general as our enemies; And even after the Lord had manifested his forgiving mercy to me, I still felt at time an uneasy distrust and shyness towards them; but on that day the Lord removed all my prejudices; for which I bless his holy Name.

In the month of August 1794, I went to Bristol; and from thence Dr. Coke took me with him to Kingswood-School, where I continued to the present time, and have endeavoured to acquire the knowledge I possibly could, in order to be useful in that sphere which the blessed hand of Providence may conduct me into, if my life is spared. I have great cause to be thankful that I came to England, for I am now fully convinced, that many of these White People, instead of being enemies and oppressors of us poor Blacks, are our friends, and deliverers from slavery, as far as their ability and circumstances will admit. I have met with most affectionate treatment from the Methodists of London, Bristol, and other places which I have had an opportunity of visiting. And I must confess, that I did not believe there were upon the face of the earth a people so friendly and human as I have proved them to be. I beg leave to acknowledge the obligations I am under to Dr. Coke, Mr. Bradford, and all the Preachers and people; and I pray GOD to reward them a thousand fold for all the favours they have shewn to me in a strange land.

Published 1789

MARY PRINCE

Mary Prince (1788–?) was born a slave in Bermuda in 1788. Separated from her family, she was sold to different owners several times. In 1815 she was sold to the Woods family for $300 and taken to Antigua. There, she joined the Moravian church in 1826 without her owner's permission. In 1828 she was taken to England, but after mistreatment she absconded and was supported by the Anti-Slavery Society (ASS). She worked as a charwoman in London and was employed as a domestic servant by Thomas Pringle, secretary of the ASS. Legally she remained enslaved and dictated her autobiography so 'that good people in England might hear from a slave what a slave had felt and suffered.' Published in 1831, it was the first 'slave narrative' to be written by a woman in the English language and the only one by a woman in Britain. Here are some of Prince's first experiences of Britain.

The History of Mary Prince, a West Indian Slave

When we drew near to England, the rheumatism seized all my limbs worse than ever, and my body was dreadfully swelled. When we landed at the Tower, I shewed my flesh to my mistress, but she took no great notice of it. We were obliged to stop at the tavern till my master got a house; and a day or two after, my mistress sent me down into the wash-house to learn to wash in the English way. In the West Indies we wash with cold water—in England with hot. I told my mistress I was afraid that putting my hands first into the hot water and then into the cold, would increase the pain in my limbs. The doctor had told my mistress long before I came from the West Indies, that I was a sickly body and the washing did not agree with me. But Mrs. Wood would not release me from the tub, so I was forced to do as I could. I grew worse, and could not stand to wash. I was then forced to sit down with the tub before me, and often through pain and weakness was reduced to kneel or to sit down on the floor, to finish my task. When I complained to my mistress of this, she only got into a passion as usual, and said washing in hot water could not hurt any one;—that I was lazy and insolent, and wanted to be free of my work; but that she would make me do it. I thought her very hard on me, and my heart rose up within me. However I kept still at that time, and went down again to wash the child's things; but the English washerwomen who were at work there, when they saw that I was so ill, had pity upon me and washed them for me.

After that, when we came up to live in Leigh Street, Mrs. Wood sorted out five bags of clothes which we had used at sea, and also such as had been worn since we came on shore, for me and the cook to wash. Elizabeth the cook told her, that she did not think that I was able to stand to the tub, and that she had better hire a woman. I also said myself, that I had come over to nurse the child, and that I was sorry I had come from Antigua, since mistress would work me so hard, without compassion for my rheumatism. Mr. and Mrs. Wood, when they heard this, rose up in a passion against me. They opened the door and bade me get out. But I was a stranger, and did not know one door in the street from another, and was unwilling to go away. They made a dreadful uproar, and from that day they constantly kept cursing and abusing me. I was obliged to wash, though I was very ill. Mrs. Wood, indeed once hired a washerwoman, but she was not well treated, and would come no more.

My master quarrelled with me another time, about one of our great washings, his wife having stirred him up to do so. He said he would compel me to do the whole of the washing given out to me, or if I again refused, he would take a short course with me: he would either send me down to the brig in the river, to carry me back to Antigua, or he would turn me at once out of doors, and let me provide for myself. I said I would willingly go back, if he would let me purchase my own freedom. But this enraged him more than all the rest: he cursed and swore at me dreadfully, and said he would never sell my freedom—if I wished to be free, I was free in England, and I might go and try what freedom would do for me, and be d——d. My heart was very sore with this treatment, but I had to go on. I continued to do my work, and did all I could to give satisfaction, but all would not do.

Shortly after, the cook left them, and then matters went on ten times worse. I always washed the child's clothes without being commanded to do it, and any thing else that was wanted in the family; though still I was very sick—very sick indeed. When the great washing came round, which was every two months, my mistress got together again a great many heavy things, such as bed-ticks, bed-coverlets, &c. for me to wash. I told her I was too ill to wash such heavy things that day. She said, she supposed I thought myself a free woman, but I was not; and if I did not do it directly I should be instantly turned out of doors. I stood a long time before I could answer, for I did not know well what to do. I knew that I was free in England, but I did not know where to go, or how to get my living; and therefore, I did not like to leave the house. But Mr. Wood said he would send for a constable to thrust me out; and at last I took courage and resolved that I would not be longer thus treated, but would go and trust to Providence. This was the fourth time they had threatened to turn me out, and, go where I might, I was determined now to take them at their word; though I thought it very hard, after I had lived with them for thirteen years, and worked for them like a horse, to be driven out in this way, like a beggar. My only fault was being sick, and therefore unable to please my mistress, who thought she never could get work enough out of her slaves; and I told them so: but they only abused me and drove me out. This took place from two to three months, I think, after we came to England.

When I came away, I went to the man (one Mash) who used to black the shoes of the family, and asked his wife to get somebody to go with me to Hatton Garden to the Moravian Missionaries:

these were the only persons I knew in England. The woman sent a young girl with me to the mission house, and I saw there a gentleman called Mr. Moore. I told him my whole story, and how my owners had treated me, and asked him to take in my trunk with what few clothes I had. The missionaries were very kind to me—they were sorry for my destitute situation, and gave me leave to bring my things to be placed under their care. They were very good people, and they told me to come to the church.

When I went back to Mr. Wood's to get my trunk, I saw a lady, Mrs. Pell, who was on a visit to my mistress. When Mr. and Mrs. Wood heard me come in, they set this lady to stop me, finding that they had gone too far with me. Mrs. Pell came out to me, and said, "Are you really going to leave, Molly? Don't leave, but come into the country with me." I believe she said this because she thought Mrs. Wood would easily get me back again. I replied to her, "Ma'am, this is the fourth time my master and mistress have driven me out, or threatened to drive me—and I will give them no more occasion to bid me go. I was not willing to leave them, for I am a stranger in this country, but now I must go—I can stay no longer to be so used." Mrs. Pell then went up stairs to my mistress, and told that I would go, and that she could not stop me. Mrs. Wood was very much hurt and frightened when she found I was determined to go out that day. She said, "If she goes the people will rob her, and then turn her adrift." She did not say this to me, but she spoke it loud enough for me to hear; that it might induce me not to go, I suppose. Mr. Wood also asked me where I was going to. I told him where I had been, and that I should never have gone away had I not been driven out by my owners. He had given me a written paper some time before, which said that I had come with them to England by my own desire; and that was true. It said also that I left them of my own free will, because I was a free woman in England; and that I was idle and would not do my work—which was not true. I gave this paper afterwards to a gentleman who inquired into my case.

I went into the kitchen and got my clothes out. The nurse and the servant girl were there, and I said to the man who was going to take out my trunk, "Stop, before you take up this trunk, and hear what I have to say before these people. I am going out of this house, as I was ordered; but I have done no wrong at all to my owners, neither here nor in the West Indies. I always worked very hard to please them, both by night and day; but there was no giving satisfaction, for my mistress could never be satisfied

63

with reasonable service. I told my mistress I was sick, and yet she has ordered me out of doors. This is the fourth time; and now I am going out."

And so I came out, and went and carried my trunk to the Moravians. I then returned back to Mash the shoe-black's house, and begged his wife to take me in. I had a little West Indian money in my trunk; and they got it changed for me. This helped to support me for a little while. The man's wife was very kind to me. I was very sick, and she boiled nourishing things up for me. She also sent for a doctor to see me, and he sent me medicine, which did me good, though I was ill for a long time with the rheumatic pains. I lived a good many months with these poor people, and they nursed me, and did all that lay in their power to serve me. The man was well acquainted with my situation, as he used to go to and fro to Mr. Wood's house to clean shoes and knives; and he and his wife were sorry for me.

About this time, a woman of the name of Hill told me of the Anti-Slavery Society, and went with me to their office, to inquire if they could do any thing to get me my freedom, and send me back to the West Indies. The gentlemen of the Society took me to a lawyer, who examined very strictly into my case; but told me that the laws of England could do nothing to make me free in Antigua. However they did all they could for me: they gave me a little money from time to time to keep me from want; and some of them went to Mr. Wood to try to persuade him to let me return a free woman to my husband; but though they offered him, as I have heard, a large sum for my freedom, he was sulky and obstinate, and would not consent to let me go free.

This was the first winter I spent in England, and I suffered much from the severe cold, and from the rheumatic pains, which still at times torment me.

Published 1831

MARY SEACOLE

Mary Seacole (1805–1881) was born Mary Jane Grant in Jamaica to a Scottish lieutenant in the British army and a Jamaican woman. From her mother she learned the use of herbal remedies and hygiene, but she also learned other medical skills from military and naval surgeons in Jamaica. She travelled widely, had considerable experience of life and treated patients suffering from a variety of ailments. She is best known for treating British troops during the Crimean War. Although initially rejected by Florence Nightingale and the War Office, she made her own way to the front line and opened 'an hotel for invalids.' When the war ended, Seacole was bankrupt and several senior military figures and the Prince of Wales raised funds for her. In 1857 she published her autobiography, a rare achievement, and later in life she increasingly moved amongst the London elite. The following extract presents her impressions of London and the challenges she faced before she left for the Crimea.

Wonderful Adventures of
Mrs. Seacole in Many Lands

As I grew into womanhood, I began to indulge that longing to travel which will never leave me while I have health and vigour. I was never weary of tracing upon an old map the route to England; and never followed with my gaze the stately ships homeward bound without longing to be in them, and see the blue hills of Jamaica fade into the distance. At that time it seemed most improbable that these girlish wishes should be gratified; but circumstances, which I need not explain, enabled me to accompany some relatives to England while I was yet a very young woman.

I shall never forget my first impressions of London. Of course, I am not going to bore the reader with them; but they are as vivid now as though the year 18—(I had very nearly let my age slip then) had not been long ago numbered with the past. Strangely enough, some of the most vivid of my recollections are the efforts of the London street-boys to poke fun at my and my companion's complexion. I am only a little brown—a few shades duskier than the brunettes whom you all admire so much; but my companion was very dark, and a fair (if I can apply the term to her) subject for their rude wit. She was hot-tempered, poor thing! and as there were no policemen to awe the boys and turn our servants' heads in those days, our progress through the London streets was sometimes a rather chequered one.

[. . .]

So I made long and unwearied application at the War Office, in blissful ignorance of the labour and time I was throwing away. I have reason to believe that I considerably interfered with the repose of sundry messengers, and disturbed, to an alarming degree, the official gravity of some nice gentlemanly young fellows, who were working out their salaries in an easy, off-hand way. But my ridiculous endeavours to gain an interview with the Secretary-at-War of course failed, and glad at last to oblige a distracted messenger, I transferred my attentions to the Quartermaster-General's department. Here I saw another gentleman, who listened to me with a great deal of polite enjoyment, and—his amusement ended—hinted, had I not better apply to the Medical Department; and accordingly I attached myself to their quarters with the same unwearying ardour. But, of course, I grew tired at last, and then I changed my plans.

Now, I am not for a single instant going to blame the authorities who would not listen to the offer of a motherly yellow woman to go to the Crimea and nurse her "sons" there, suffering from cholera, diarrhœa, and a host of lesser ills. In my country, where people know our use, it would have been different; but here it was natural enough—although I had references, and other voices spoke for me—that they should laugh, good-naturedly enough, at my offer. War, I know, is a serious game, but sometimes very humble actors are of great use in it, and if the reader, when he comes in time to peruse the evidence of those who had to do with the Sebastopol drama, of my share in it, will turn back to this chapter, he will confess perhaps that, after all, the impulse which led me to the War Department was not unnatural.

My new scheme was, I candidly confess, worse devised than the one which had failed. Miss Nightingale had left England for the Crimea, but other nurses were still to follow, and my new plan was simply to offer myself to Mrs. H——as a recruit. Feeling that I was one of the very women they most wanted, experienced and fond of the work, I jumped at once to the conclusion that they would gladly enrol me in their number. To go to Cox's, the army agents, who were most obliging to me, and obtain the Secretary-at-War's private address, did not take long; and that done, I laid the same pertinacious siege to his great house in——Square, as I had previously done to his place of business.

Many a long hour did I wait in his great hall, while scores passed in and out; many of them looking curiously at me. The flunkeys, noble creatures! marvelled exceedingly at the yellow woman whom no excuses could get rid of, nor impertinence dismay, and showed me very clearly that they resented my persisting in remaining there in mute appeal from their sovereign will. At last I gave that up, after a message from Mrs. H. that the full complement of nurses had been secured, and that my offer could not be entertained. Once again I tried, and had an interview this time with one of Miss Nightingale's companions. She gave me the same reply, and I read in her face the fact, that had there been a vacancy, I should not have been chosen to fill it.

As a last resort, I applied to the managers of the Crimean Fund to know whether they would give me a passage to the camp—once there I would trust to something turning up. But this failed also, and one cold evening I stood in the twilight, which was fast deepening into wintry night, and looked back upon the ruins of my last castle in the air. The disappointment seemed a cruel one. I was so conscious of the unselfishness of the motives which induced me to leave England—so certain of the service I could render among the sick soldiery, and yet I found it so difficult to convince others of these facts. Doubts and suspicions arose in my heart for the first and last time, thank Heaven. Was it possible that American prejudices against colour had some root here? Did these ladies shrink from accepting my aid because my blood flowed beneath a somewhat duskier skin than theirs? Tears streamed down my foolish cheeks, as I stood in the fast thinning streets; tears of grief that any should doubt my motives—that Heaven should deny me the opportunity that I sought. Then I stood still, and looking upward through and through the dark clouds that shadowed London, prayed aloud for help. I dare say that I was a strange sight to the few passers-by, who hastened homeward through the gloom and mist of that wintry night. I dare say those who read these pages will wonder at me as much as they who saw me did; but you must all remember that I am one of an impulsive people, and find it hard to put that restraint upon my feelings which to you is so easy and natural.

Published 1857

LINDA BRENT

Linda Brent was the pseudonym of Harriet Jacobs (1813–1897), who became the first formerly enslaved African American woman to write an autobiography. Jacobs was born into slavery in North Carolina and, like many enslaved women, suffered sexual harassment from her owner. Her autobiography not only details this abuse but also her unusual relationship with a wealthy white lawyer, who became the father of her two children, her seven years in hiding and separation from her children and subsequently her audacious escape and liberation in 1842. Jacobs settled in New York, but was forced to move several times as her former owner continually sought to re-enslave her. Jacobs later became connected with the abolitionist movement, but it is evident that she agonized for several years before agreeing to share details of her private life in her autobiography. Her writing also includes her description of the journey she made to England in 1845 as part of her employment as a children's nanny.

Incidents in the Life of a Slave Girl

We sailed from New York, and arrived in Liverpool after a pleasant voyage of twelve days. We proceeded directly to London, and took lodgings at the Adelaide Hotel. The supper seemed to me less luxurious than those I had seen in American hotels; but my situation was indescribably more pleasant. For the first time in my life I was in a place where I was treated according to my deportment, without reference to my complexion. I felt as if a great millstone had been lifted from my breast. Ensconced in a pleasant room, with my dear little charge, I laid my head on my pillow, for the first time, with the delightful consciousness of pure, unadulterated freedom.

As I had constant care of the child, I had little opportunity to see the wonders of that great city; but I watched the tide of life that flowed through the streets, and found it a strange contrast to the stagnation in our Southern towns. Mr. Bruce took his little daughter to spend some days with friends in Oxford Crescent, and of course it was necessary for me to accompany her. I had heard much of the systematic method of English education, and I was very desirous that my dear Mary should steer straight in the midst of so much propriety. I closely observed her little playmates and their nurses, being ready to take any lessons in the science of good management. The children were more rosy than American children, but I did not see that they differed materially in other respects. They were like all children— sometimes docile and sometimes wayward.

We next went to Steventon, in Berkshire. It was a small town, said to be the poorest in the county. I saw men working in the fields for six shillings, and seven shillings, a week, and women for sixpence, and sevenpence, a day, out of which they boarded themselves. Of course they lived in the most primitive manner; it could not be otherwise, where a woman's wages for an entire day were not sufficient to buy a pound of meat. They paid very low rents, and their clothes were made of the cheapest fabrics, though much better than could have been procured in the United States for the same money. I had heard much about the oppression of the poor in Europe. The people I saw around me were, many of them, among the poorest poor. But when I visited them in their little thatched cottages, I felt that the condition of even the meanest and most ignorant among them was vastly superior to the condition of the most favored slaves in America. They labored hard; but they were not ordered out to toil while the stars were in the sky, and driven and slashed by an overseer, through heat and cold, till the stars shone out again.

Their homes were very humble; but they were protected by law. No insolent patrols could come, in the dead of night, and flog them at their pleasure. The father, when he closed his cottage door, felt safe with his family around him. No master or overseer could come and take from his wife, or his daughter. They must separate to earn their living; but the parents knew where their children were going, and could communicate with them by letters. The relations of husband and wife, parent and child, were too sacred for the richest noble in the land to violate with impunity. Much was being done to enlighten these poor people. Schools were established among them, and benevolent societies were active in efforts to ameliorate their condition. There was no law forbidding them to learn to read and write; and if they helped each other in spelling out the Bible, they were in no danger of thirty-nine lashes, as was the case with myself and poor, pious, old uncle Fred. I repeat that the most ignorant and the most destitute of these peasants was a thousand fold better off than the most pampered American slave.

I do not deny that the poor are oppressed in Europe. I am not disposed to paint their condition so rose-colored as the Hon. Miss Murray paints the condition of the slaves in the United States. A small portion of *my* experience would enable her to read her own pages with anointed eyes. If she were to lay aside her title, and, instead of visiting among the fashionable, become domesticated, as a poor governess, on some plantation in Louisiana or Alabama, she would see and hear things that would make her tell quite a different story.

My visit to England is a memorable event in my life, from the fact of my having there received strong religious impressions. The contemptuous manner in which the communion had been administered to colored people, in my native place; the church membership of Dr. Flint, and others like him; and the buying and selling of slaves, by professed ministers of the gospel, had given me a prejudice against the Episcopal church. The whole service seemed to me a mockery and a sham. But my home in Steventon was in the family of a clergyman, who was a true disciple of Jesus. The beauty of his daily life inspired me with faith in the genuineness of Christian professions. Grace entered my heart, and I knelt at the communion table, I trust, in true humility of soul.

I remained abroad ten months, which was much longer than I had anticipated. During all that time, I never saw the slightest symptom of prejudice against color. Indeed, I entirely forgot it, till the time came for us to return to America.

Published 1861

FREDERICK DOUGLASS

Frederick Douglass (*c.*1817–1895) was born into slavery as Frederick Bailey in Maryland, USA. He believed that his owner was also his father and from a young age was determined to free himself from slavery; this he did in 1838. Douglass soon joined the abolitionist movement and eventually became one of its leading figures and the most prominent African American in the nineteenth century. He was largely self-educated and produced the first and most famous version of this autobiography, *Narrative of the Life of Frederick Douglass, An American Slave* in 1845. It immediately became a bestseller, and Douglass later published two other expanded autobiographies. In the same year, Douglass made his first tour of Britain and Ireland and spoke throughout the British Isles for the next two years. Douglass fought for the rights of African Americans throughout his life, as well as embracing women's suffrage, Irish Nationalism and temperance. Here's a description of some of his experiences in England and Scotland during his first visit, from his second autobiography, *My Bondage and My Freedom*.

My Bondage and My Freedom

The second day after my arrival at Liverpool, in company with my friend, Buffum, and several other friends, I went to Eaton Hall, the residence of the Marquis of Westminster, one of the most splendid buildings in England. On approaching the door, I found several of our American passengers, who came out with us in the Cambria, waiting for admission, as but one party was allowed in the house at a time. We all had to wait till the company within came out. And of all the faces, expressive of chagrin, those of the Americans were preeminent. They looked as sour as vinegar, and as bitter as gall, when they found I was to be admitted on equal terms with themselves. When the door was opened, I walked in, on an equal footing with my white fellow-citizens, and from all I could see, I had as much attention paid me by the servants that showed us through the house, as any with a paler skin. As I walked through the building, the statuary did not fall down, the pictures did not leap from their places, the doors did not refuse to open, and the servants did not say, '*We don't allow niggers in here!*'

"A happy new-year to you, and all the friends of freedom."

My time and labors, while abroad, were divided

between England, Ireland, Scotland, and Wales. Upon this experience alone, I might write a book twice the size of this, "*My Bondage and my Freedom.*" I visited and lectured in nearly all the large towns and cities in the United Kingdom, and enjoyed many favorable opportunities for observation and information. But books on England are abundant, and the public may, therefore, dismiss any fear that I am meditating another infliction in that line; though, in truth, I should like much to write a book on those countries, if for nothing else, to make grateful mention of the many dear friends, whose benevolent actions toward me are ineffaceably stamped upon my memory, and warmly treasured in my heart. To these friends I owe my freedom in the United States. On their own motion, without any solicitation from me, (Mrs. Henry Richardson, a clever lady, remarkable for her devotion to every good work, taking the lead,) they raised a fund sufficient to purchase my freedom, and actually paid it over, and placed the papers of my manumission in my hands, before they would tolerate the idea of my returning to this, my native country. To this commercial transaction I owe my exemption from the democratic operation of the fugitive slave bill of 1850. But for this, I might at any time become a victim of this most cruel and scandalous enactment, and be doomed to end my life, as I began it, a slave. The sum paid for my freedom was one hundred and fifty pounds sterling.

[. . .]

But to the second circumstance, namely, the position of the Free Church of Scotland, with the great Doctors Chalmers, Cunningham, and Candlish at its head. That church, with its leaders, put it out of the power of the Scotch people to ask the old question, which we in the north have often most wickedly asked—"*What have we to do with slavery?*" That church had taken the price of blood into its treasury, with which to build *free* churches, and to pay *free* church ministers for preaching the gospel; and, worse still, when honest John Murray, of Bowlien Bay—now gone to his reward in heaven—with William Smeal, Andrew Paton, Frederick Card, and other sterling anti-slavery men in Glasgow, denounced the transaction as disgraceful and shocking to the religious sentiment of Scotland, this church, through its leading divines, instead of repenting and seeking to mend the mistake into which it had fallen, made it a flagrant sin, by undertaking to defend, in the name of God and the bible, the principle not only of taking the money of slave-dealers to build churches, but of holding fellowship with the holders and traffickers in human flesh. This, the reader will see, brought up the whole question of slavery, and opened the way to its full discussion, without any agency of mine. I have never seen a people more deeply moved than were the people of Scotland, on this very question. Public meeting succeeded public meeting. Speech after speech, pamphlet after pamphlet, editorial after editorial, sermon after sermon, soon lashed the conscientious Scotch people into a perfect *furore.* "SEND BACK THE MONEY!" was indignantly cried out, from Greenock to Edinburgh, and from Edinburgh to Aberdeen. George Thompson, of London, Henry C. Wright, of the United States, James N. Buffum, of Lynn, Massachusetts, and myself were on the anti-slavery side; and Doctors Chalmers, Cunningham, and Candlish on the other. In a conflict where the latter could have had even the show of right, the truth, in our hands as against them, must have been driven to the wall; and while I believe we were able to carry the conscience of the country against the action of the Free Church, the battle, it must be confessed, was a hard-fought one. Abler defenders of the doctrine of fellowshiping slaveholders as christians, have not been met with. In defending this doctrine, it was necessary to deny that slavery is a sin. If driven from this position, they were compelled to deny that slaveholders were responsible for the sin; and if driven from both these positions, they must deny that it is a sin in such a sense, and that slaveholders are sinners in such a sense, as to make it wrong, in the circumstances in which they were placed, to recognize them as christians. Dr. Cunningham was the most powerful debater on the slavery side of the question; Mr. Thompson was the ablest on the anti-slavery side. A scene occurred between these two men, a parallel to which I think I never witnessed before, and I know I never have since. The scene was caused by a single exclamation on the part of Mr. Thompson.

The general assembly of the Free Church was in progress at Cannon Mills, Edinburgh. The building would hold about twenty-five hundred persons; and on this occasion it was densely packed, notice having been given that Doctors Cunningham and Candlish would speak, that day, in defense of the relations of the Free Church of Scotland to slavery in America. Messrs. Thompson, Buffum, myself, and a few anti-slavery friends, attended, but sat at such a distance, and in such a position, that, perhaps, we were not observed from the platform. The excitement was intense, having been greatly increased by a series of meetings held by Messrs. Thompson, Wright, Buffum, and myself, in the most splendid hall in that most beautiful city, just previous to the meetings of the general assembly. "SEND BACK THE MONEY!" stared at us from every street corner; "SEND BACK THE MONEY!" in large capitals, adorned the broad flags of the pavement; "SEND BACK THE MONEY!" was the chorus of the popular street songs; "SEND BACK THE MONEY!" was the heading of leading editorials in the daily newspapers. This day, at Cannon Mills, the great doctors of the church were to give an answer to this loud and stern demand. Men of all parties and all sects were most eager to hear. Something great was expected. The occasion was great, the men great, and great speeches were expected from them.

In addition to the outside pressure upon Doctors Cunningham and Candlish, there was wavering in their own ranks. The conscience of the church itself was not ease. A dissatisfaction with the position of the church touching slavery, was sensibly manifest among the members, and something must be done to counteract this untoward influence. The great Dr. Chalmers was in feeble health, at the time. His most potent eloquence could not now be summoned to Cannon Mills, as formerly. He whose voice was able to rend asunder and dash down the granite walls of the established church of Scotland, and to lead a host in solemn procession from it, as from a doomed city, was now old and enfeebled.

Besides, he had said his word on this very question; and his word had not silenced the clamor without, nor stilled the anxious heavings within. The occasion was momentous, and felt to be so. The church was in a perilous condition. A change of some sort must take place in her condition, or she must go to pieces. To stand where she did, was impossible. The whole weight of the matter fell on Cunningham and Candlish. No shoulders in the church were broader than theirs; and I must say, badly as I detest the principles laid down and defended by them, I was compelled to acknowledge the vast mental endowments of the men. Cunningham rose; and his rising was the signal for almost tumultuous applause. You will say this was scarcely in keeping with the solemnity of the occasion, but to me it served to increase its grandeur and gravity. The applause, though tumultuous, was not joyous. It seemed to me, as it thundered up from the vast audience, like the fall of an immense shaft, flung from shoulders already galled by its crushing weight. It was like saying, "Doctor, we have borne this burden long enough, and willingly fling it upon you. Since it was you who brought it upon us, take it now, and do what you will with it, for we are too weary to bear it."

Doctor Cunningham proceeded with his speech, abounding in logic, learning, and eloquence, and apparently bearing down all opposition; but at the moment—the fatal moment—when he was just bringing all his arguments to a point, and that point being, that neither Jesus Christ nor his holy apostles regarded slaveholding as a sin, George Thompson, in a clear, sonorous, but rebuking voice, broke the deep stillness of the audience, exclaiming, "HEAR! HEAR! HEAR!" The effect of this simple and common exclamation is almost incredible. It was as if a granite wall had been suddenly flung up against the advancing current of a mighty river. For a moment, speaker and audience were brought to a dead silence. Both the doctor and his hearers seemed appalled by the audacity, as well as the fitness of the rebuke. At length a shout went up to the cry of "*Put him out!*" Happily, no one attempted to execute this cowardly order, and the doctor proceeded with his discourse. Not, however, as before, did the learned doctor proceed. The exclamation of Thompson must have reëchoed itself a thousand times in his memory, during the remainder of his speech, for the doctor never recovered from the blow.

The deed was done, however; the pillars of the church—*the proud, Free Church of Scotland*—were committed, and the humility of repentance was absent. The Free Church held on to the blood-stained money, and continued to justify itself in its position—and of course to apologize for slavery—and does so till this day. She lost a glorious opportunity for giving her voice, her vote, and her example to the cause of humanity; and to-day she is staggering under the curse of the enslaved, whose blood is in her skirts. The people of Scotland are, to this day, deeply grieved at the course pursued by the Free Church, and would hail, as a relief from a deep and blighting shame, the "sending back the money" to the slaveholders from whom it was gathered.

One good result followed the conduct of the Free Church; it furnished an occasion for making the people of Scotland thoroughly acquainted with the character of slavery, and for arraying against the system the moral and religious sentiment of that country. Therefore, while we did not succeed in accomplishing the specific object of our mission, namely—procure the sending back of the money—we were amply justified by the good which really did result from our labors.

Published 1855

WILLIAM WELLS BROWN

William Wells Brown (1814–1884) was born enslaved in Kentucky, USA, but escaped from slavery in 1834. Adopting his new surname, he was active in the Underground Railroad and as an abolitionist lecturer and campaigner. Influenced by Frederick Douglass, and, like him, also self-taught, he published his *Narrative of William Wells Brown, A Fugitive Slave* in 1847. In 1849 he made his first visit to Britain and Ireland where he became an important abolitionist speaker. He remained in Europe for three years and first published his reflections on these travels in 1852. Brown later wrote plays as well as historical works and he became the first African American to write a novel with the 1853 publication of *Clotel: or The President's Daughter*. In the following extracts, he reflects on his various experiences in Britain.

The American Fugitive in Europe: Sketches of Places and People Abroad

No person of my complexion can visit this country without being struck with the marked difference between the English and the Americans. The prejudice which I have experienced on all and every occasion in the United States, and to some extent on board the *Canada*, vanished as soon as I set foot on the soil of Britain. In America I had been bought and sold as a slave in the Southern States. In the so-called Free States, I had been treated as one born to occupy an inferior position,—in steamers, compelled to take my fare on the deck; in hotels, to take my meals in the kitchen; in coaches, to ride on the outside; in railways, to ride in the "negrocar;" and in churches, to sit in the "negro-pew." But no sooner was I on British soil, than I was recognized as a man, and an equal. The very dogs in the streets appeared conscious of my manhood. Such is the difference, and such is the change that is brought about by a trip of nine days in an Atlantic steamer.

I was not more struck with the treatment of the people than with the appearance of the great seaport of the world. The gray stone piers and docks, the dark look of the magnificent warehouses, the substantial appearance of everything around, causes one to think himself in a new world instead of the old. Everything in Liverpool looks old, yet nothing is worn out. The beautiful villas on the opposite side of the river, in the vicinity of Birkenhead, together with the countless number of vessels in the river, and the great ships to be seen in the stream, give life and animation to the whole scene.

Everything in and about Liverpool seems to be built for the future as well as the present. We had time to examine but few of the public buildings, the first of which was the custom-house, an edifice that would be an ornament to any city in the world.

[. . .]

We reached London at mid-day, where I was soon comfortably lodged at 22 Cecil-street, Strand. As it was three o'clock, I lost no time in seeking out a dining saloon, which I had no difficulty in finding in the Strand. It being the first house of the kind I had entered in London, I was not a little annoyed at the politeness of the waiter. The first salutation I had, after seating myself in one of the stalls, was, "Ox tail, sir; gravy soup; carrot soup, sir; roast beef; roast pork; boiled beef; roast lamb; boiled leg of mutton, sir, with caper sauce; jugged hare, sir; boiled knuckle of veal and bacon; roast turkey and oyster sauce; sucking pig, sir; curried chicken; harrico mutton, sir." These, and many other dishes, which I have forgotten, were called over with a rapidity that would have done credit to one of our Yankee pedlers in crying his wares in a New England village. I was so completely taken by surprise, that I asked for a "bill of fare," and told him to leave me. No city in the world furnishes a cheaper, better, and quicker meal for the weary traveller, than a London eating-house.

A few days after my arrival in London, I received an invitation from John Lee, Esq., LL.D., whom I had met at the Peace Congress in Paris, to pay him a visit at his seat, near Aylesbury; and as the time was "fixed" by the doctor, I took the train on the appointed day, on my way to Hartwell House.

I had heard much of the aristocracy of England, and must confess that I was not a little prejudiced against them. On a bright sunshiny day, between the hours of twelve and two, I found myself seated in a carriage, my back turned upon Aylesbury, the vehicle whirling rapidly over the smooth macadamised road, and I on my first visit to an English gentleman. Twenty minutes' ride, and a turn to the right, and we were amid the fine old trees of Hartwell Park; one having suspended from its branches the national banners of several different countries, among them the "Stars and Stripes." I felt glad that my own country's flag had a place there, although Campbell's lines—

> "United States, your banner wears
> Two emblems,—one of fame;
> Alas! the other that it bears
> Reminds us of your shame!
> The white man's liberty in types
> Stands blazoned by your stars;
> But what's the meaning of your stripes?—
> They mean your Negro-scars"—

were at the time continually running through my mind. Arrived at the door, and we received what every one does who visits Dr. Lee—a hearty welcome. I was immediately shown into a room with a lofty ceiling, hung round with fine specimens of the Italian masters, and told that this was my apartment. Hartwell House stands in an extensive park, shaded with trees that made me think of the oaks and elms in an American forest, and many of whose limbs had been trimmed and nursed with the best of care. This was for several years the residence of John Hampden the patriot, and more recently that of Louis XVIII., during his exile in this country. The house is built on a very extensive scale, and is ornamented in the interior with carvings in wood of many of the kings and princes of bygone centuries. A room some sixty feet by twenty-five contains a variety of articles that the doctor has collected together—the whole forming a museum that would be considered a sight in the Western States of America.

The morning after my arrival at Hartwell I was up at an early hour—in fact, before any of the servants—wandering about through the vast halls, and trying to find my way out; in which I eventually succeeded, but not, however, without aid. It had rained the previous night, and the sun was peeping through a misty cloud as I strolled through the park, listening to the sweet voices of the birds that were fluttering in the tops of the trees, and trimming their wings for a morning flight. The silence of the night had not yet been broken by the voice of man; and I wandered about the vast park unannoyed, except by the dew from the grass that wet my slippers. Not far from the house I came abruptly upon a beautiful little pond of water, where the gold-fish were flouncing about, and the gentle ripples glittering in the sunshine looked like so many silver minnows playing on the surface.

While strolling about with pleasure, and only regretting that my dear daughters were not with me to enjoy the morning's walk, I saw the gardener on his way to the garden. I followed him, and was soon feasting my eyes upon the richest specimens of garden scenery. There were the peaches hanging upon the trees that were fastened to the wall; vegetables, fruit and flowers, were there in all their bloom and beauty; and even the variegated geranium of a warmer clime was there in its hothouse home, and seemed to have forgotten that it was in a different country from its own. Dr. Lee shows great taste in the management of his garden. I have seldom seen a more splendid variety of fruits and flowers in the Southern States of America than I saw at Hartwell House.

I should, however, state that I was not the only guest at Hartwell during my stay. Dr. Lee had invited several others of the American delegation to the Peace Congress, and two or three of the French delegates, who were on a visit to England, were enjoying the doctor's hospitality. Dr. Lee is a stanch friend of Temperance, as well as of the cause of universal freedom. Every year he treats his tenantry to a dinner, and I need not add that these are always conducted on the principle of total abstinence.

During the second day we visited several of the cottages of the work-people, and in these I took no little interest. The people of the United States know nothing of the real condition of the laboring classes of England. The peasants of Great Britain are always spoken of as belonging to the soil. I was taught in America that the English laborer was no better off than the slave upon a Carolina rice-field. I had seen the slaves in Missouri huddled together, three, four, and even five families in a single room, not more than fifteen by twenty-five feet square, and I expected to see the same in England. But in this I was disappointed. After visiting a new house that the doctor was building, he took us into one of the cottages that stood near the road, and gave us an opportunity of seeing, for the first time, an English peasant's cot. We entered a low, whitewashed room, with a stone floor that showed an admirable degree of cleanness. Before us was a row of shelves filled with earthen dishes and pewter spoons, glittering as if they had just come from under the hand of a woman of taste. A "Cobden loaf" of bread, that had just been left by the baker's boy, lay upon an oaken table which had been much worn away with the scrubbing-brush; while just above lay the old family Bible, that had been handed down from father to son, until its possession was considered of almost as great value as its contents. A half-open door, leading into another room, showed us a clean bed; the whole presenting as fine a picture of neatness, order and comfort, as the most fastidious taste could wish to see. No occupant was present, and therefore I inspected everything with a greater degree of freedom. "In front of the cottage was a small grass-plot, with here and there a bed of flowers, cheated out of its share of sunshine by the tall holly that had been planted near it." As I looked upon the home of the laborer, my thoughts were with my enslaved countrymen. What a difference, thought I, there is between the tillers of the soil in England and America! There could not be a more complete refutation of the assertion that the English laborer is no better off than the American slave, than the scenes that were then before me. I called the attention of one of my American friends to a beautiful rose near the door of the cot, and said to him, "The law that will protect that flower will also guard and protect the hand that planted it." He knew that I had drank deep of the cup of slavery, was aware of what I meant, and merely nodded his head in reply. I never experienced hospitality more genuine, and yet more unpretending, than was meted out to me while at Hartwell. And the favorable impression made on my own mind by the distinguished proprietor of Hartwell Park was nearly as indelible as my humble name that the doctor had engraven in a brick, in a vault beneath the Observatory in Hartwell House.

On my return to London I accepted an invitation to join a party on a visit to Windsor Castle; and, taking the train at the Waterloo Bridge Station, we were soon passing through a pleasant part of the country. Arrived at the castle, we committed ourselves into the hands of the servants, and were introduced into Her Majesty's State Apartments, Audience Chamber, Vandyck Room, Waterloo Chambers, Gold Pantry, and many others whose names I have forgotten. In wandering about the different apartments I lost my company, and in trying to find them passed through a room in which hung a magnificent portrait of Charles I., by Vandyck. The hum and noise of my companions had ceased, and I had the scene and silence to myself. I looked in vain for the king's evil genius (Cromwell), but he was not in the same room. The pencil of Sir Peter Lely has left a splendid full-length likeness of James II. George IV. is suspended from a peg in the wall, looking as if it was fresh from the hands of Sir Thomas Lawrence, its admirable painter. I was now in St. George's Hall, and I gazed upward to view the beautiful figures on the ceiling until my neck was nearly out of joint. Leaving this room, I inspected with interest the ancient *keep* of the castle. In past centuries this part of the palace was used as a prison. Here James the First of Scotland was detained a prisoner for eighteen years. I viewed the window through which the young prince had often looked to catch a glimpse of the young and beautiful Lady Jane, daughter of the Earl of Somerset, with whom he was enamored.

From the top of the Round Tower I had a fine view of the surrounding country. Stoke Park, once the residence of that great friend of humanity and civilization, William Penn, was among the scenes that I beheld with pleasure from Windsor Castle. Four years ago, when in the city of Philadelphia, and hunting up the places associated with the name of this distinguished man, and more recently when walking over the farm once occupied by him, examining the old malt-house which is now left standing, because of the veneration with which the name of the man who built it is held, I had no idea that I should ever see the dwelling which he had occupied in the Old World. Stoke Park is about four miles from Windsor, and is now owned by the Right Hon. Henry Labouchere.

The castle, standing as it does on an eminence, and surrounded by a beautiful valley covered with splendid villas, has a most magnificent appearance. It rears its massive towers and irregular walls over and above every other object. How full this old palace is of material for thought! How one could ramble here alone, or with one or two congenial companions, and enjoy a recapitulation of its history! But an engagement to be at Croydon in the evening cut short my stay at Windsor, and compelled me to return to town in advance of my party.

Having met with John Morland, Esq., at Paris, he gave me an invitation to visit Croydon, and deliver a lecture on American Slavery; and last evening, at eight o'clock, I found myself in a fine old building in the town, and facing the first English audience that I had seen in the sea-girt isle. It was my first welcome in England. The assembly was an enthusiastic one, and made still more so by the appearance of George Thompson, Esq., M. P., upon the platform. It is not my intention to give accounts of my lectures or meetings in these pages. I therefore merely say that I left Croydon with a good impression of the English, and Heath Lodge with a feeling that its occupant was one of the most benevolent of men.

The same party with whom I visited Windsor being supplied with a card of admission to the Bank of England, I accepted an invitation to be one of the company. We entered the vast building at a little past twelve o'clock. The sun threw into the large halls a brilliancy that seemed to light up the countenances of the almost countless number of clerks, who were at their desks, or serving persons at the counters. As nearly all my countrymen who visit London pay their respects to this noted institution, I shall sum up my visit to it by saying that it surpassed my highest idea of a bank. But a stroll through this monster building of gold and silver brought to my mind an incident with which I was connected a year after my escape from slavery.

[. . .]

I have devoted the past ten days to sight-seeing in the metropolis, the first two of which were spent in the British Museum. After procuring a guide-book at the door as I entered, I seated myself on the first seat that caught my eye, arranged as well as I could in my mind the different rooms, and then commenced in good earnest. The first part I visited was the gallery of antiquities, through to the north gallery, and thence to the Lycian room. This place is filled with tombs, bas-reliefs, statues, and other productions of the same art. Venus, seated, and smelling a lotus-flower which she held in her hand, and attended by three Graces, put a stop to the rapid strides that I was making through this part of the hall. This is really one of the most precious productions of the art that I have ever seen. Many of the figures in this room are very much mutilated; yet one can linger here for hours with interest. A good number of the statues are of uncertain date; they are of great value as works of art, and more so as a means of enlightening much that has been obscure with respect to Lycia, an ancient and celebrated country of Asia Minor.

In passing through the eastern zoological gallery, I was surrounded on every side by an army of portraits suspended upon the walls; and among these was the Protector. The people of one century kicks his bones through the streets of London, another puts his portrait in the British Museum, and a future generation may possibly give him a place in Westminster Abbey. Such is the uncertainty of the human character. Yesterday, a common soldier; to-day, the ruler of an empire; tomorrow, suspended upon the gallows. In an adjoining room I saw a portrait of Baxter, which gives one a pretty good idea of the great nonconformist. In the same room hung a splendid modern portrait, without any intimation in the guide-book of who it represented, or when it was painted. It was so much like one whom I had seen, and on whom my affections were placed in my younger days, that I obtained a seat from an adjoining room and rested myself before it. After sitting half an hour or more, I wandered to another part of the building, but only to return again to my "first love," where I remained till the throng had disappeared, one after another, and the officer reminded me that it was time to close.

It was eight o'clock before I reached my lodgings. Although fatigued by the day's exertions, I again resumed the reading of Roscoe's "Leo X.," and had nearly finished seventy-three pages, when the clock on St. Martin's Church apprised me that it was two. He who escapes from slavery at the age of twenty years, without any education, as did the writer of this, must read when others are asleep, if he would catch up with the rest of the world. "To be wise," says Pope, "is but to know how little can be known." The true searcher after truth and knowledge is always like a child; although gaining strength from year to year, he still "learns to labor and to wait." The field of labor is ever expanding before him, reminding him that he has yet more to learn; teaching him that he is nothing more than a child in knowledge, and inviting him onward with a thousand varied charms. The son may take possession of the father's goods at his death, but he cannot inherit with the property the father's cultivated mind. He may put on the father's old coat, but that is all; the immortal mind of the first wearer has gone to the tomb. Property may be bequeathed, but knowledge cannot. Then let him who would be useful in his day and generation be up and doing. Like the

Chinese student who learned perseverance from the woman whom he saw trying to rub a crow-bar into a needle, so should we take the experience of the past to lighten our feet through the paths of the future.

The next morning, at ten, I was again at the door of the great building; was soon within its walls seeing what time would not allow of the previous day. I spent some hours in looking through glass cases, viewing specimens of minerals such as can scarcely be found in any place out of the British Museum. During this day I did not fail to visit the great library. It is a spacious room, surrounded with large glass cases filled with volumes whose very look tells you that they are of age. Around, under the cornice, were arranged a number of old, black-looking portraits, in all probability the authors of some of the works in the glass cases beneath. About the room were placed long tables, with stands for reading and writing, and around these were a number of men busily engaged in looking over some chosen author. Old men with gray hairs, young men with moustaches, some in cloth, others in fustian,—indicating that men of different rank can meet here. Not a single word was spoken during my stay; all appearing to enjoy the silence that reigned throughout the great room. This is indeed a retreat from the world. No one inquires who the man is that is at his side, and each pursues in silence his own researches. The racing of pens over the sheets of paper was all that disturbed the stillness of the occasion.

From the library I strolled to other rooms, and feasted my eyes on what I had never before seen. He who goes over this immense building cannot do so without a feeling of admiration for the men whose energy has brought together this vast and wonderful collection of things, the like of which cannot be found in any other museum in the world. The reflection of the setting sun against a mirror in one of the rooms told me that night was approaching, and I had but a moment in which to take another look at the portrait that I had seen on the previous day, and then bade adieu to the museum.

Having published the narrative of my life and escape from slavery, and put it into the booksellers' hands, and seeing a prospect of a fair sale, I ventured to take from my purse the last sovereign to make up a small sum to remit to the United States, for the support of my daughters, who are at school there. Before doing this, however, I had made arrangements to attend a public meeting in the city of Worcester, at which the mayor was to preside. Being informed by the friends of the slave there that I would in all probability sell a number of copies of my book, and being told that Worcester was only ten miles from London, I felt safe in parting with all but a few shillings, feeling sure that my purse would soon be again replenished. But you may guess my surprise, when I learned that Worcester was above a hundred miles from London, and that I had not retained money enough to defray my expenses to the place. In my haste and wish to make up the ten pounds to send to my children, I had forgotten that the payment for my lodgings would be demanded before I should leave town. Saturday morning came; I paid my lodging-bill, and had three shillings and fourpence left; and out of this sum I was to get three dinners, as I was only served with breakfast and tea at my lodgings.

Nowhere in the British empire do the people witness as dark days as in London. It was on Monday morning, in the fore part of October, as the clock on St. Martin's Church was striking ten, that I left my lodgings, and turned into the Strand. The street-lamps were yet burning, and the shops were all lighted, as if day had not made its appearance. This great thoroughfare, as usual at this time of the day, was thronged with business men going their way, and women sauntering about for pleasure or for the want of something better to do. I passed down the Strand to Charing Cross, and looked in vain to see the majestic statue of Nelson upon the top of the great shaft. The clock on St. Martin's Church struck eleven, but my sight could not penetrate through the dark veil that hung between its face and me. In fact, day had been completely turned into night; and the brilliant lights from the shop-windows almost persuaded me that another day had not appeared. A London fog cannot be described. To be appreciated, it must be seen, or, rather, felt, for it is altogether impossible to be clear and lucid on such a subject. It is the only thing which gives you an idea of what Milton meant when he talked of darkness visible. There is a kind of light, to be sure; but it only serves as a medium for a series of optical illusions; and, for all useful purposes of vision, the deepest darkness that ever fell from the heavens is infinitely preferable. A man perceives a coach a dozen yards off, and a single stride brings him among the horses' feet; he sees a gas-light faintly glimmering (as he thinks) at a distance, but scarcely has he advanced a step or two towards it, when he becomes convinced of its actual station by finding his head rattling against the post; and as for attempting, if you get once mystified, to distinguish one street from another, it is ridiculous to think of such a thing.

Turning, I retraced my steps, and was soon passing through the massive gates of Temple Bar, wending my way to the city, when a beggar-boy at my heels accosted me for a half-penny to buy bread. I had scarcely served the boy, when I observed near by, and standing close to a lamp-post, a colored man, and from his general appearance I was satisfied that he was an American. He eyed me attentively as I passed him, and seemed anxious to speak. When I had got some distance from him I looked back, and his eyes were still upon me. No longer able to resist the temptation to speak with him, I returned, and, commencing conversation with him, learned a little of his history, which was as follows: He had, he said, escaped from slavery in Maryland, and reached New York; but not feeling himself secure there, he had, through the kindness of the captain of an English ship, made his way to Liverpool; and not being able to get employment there, he had come up to London. Here he had met with no better success, and having been employed in the growing of tobacco, and being unaccustomed to any other work, he could not get labor in England. I told him he had better try to get to the West Indies; but he informed me that he had not a single penny, and that he had had nothing to eat that day.

By this man's story I was moved to tears, and, going to a neighboring shop. I took from my purse my last shilling, changed it, and gave this poor brother fugitive one half. The poor man burst into tears as I placed the sixpence in his hand, and said, "You are the first friend I have met in London." I bade him farewell, and left him with a feeling of regret that I could not place him beyond the reach of want. I went on my way to the city, and while going through Cheapside a streak of light appeared in the east, that reminded me that it was not night. In vain I wandered from street to street, with the hope that I might meet some one who would lend me money enough to get to Worcester. Hungry and fatigued I was returning to my lodgings, when the great clock of St. Paul's Church, under whose shadow I was then passing, struck four. A stroll through Fleet-street and the Strand, and I was again pacing my room. On my return, I found a letter from Worcester had arrived in my absence, informing me that a party of gentlemen would meet me the next day on my reaching that place, and saying, "Bring plenty of books, as you will doubtless sell a large number." The last sixpence had been spent for postage-stamps, in order to send off some letters to other places, and I could not even stamp a letter in answer to the one last from Worcester. The only vestige of money about me was a smooth farthing that a little girl had given to me at the meeting at Croydon, saying, "This is for the slaves." I was three thousand miles from home, with but a single

107

farthing in my pocket! Where on earth is a man without money more destitute? The cold hills of the Arctic regions have not a more inhospitable appearance than London to the stranger with an empty pocket. But whilst I felt depressed at being in such a sad condition, I was conscious that I had done right in remitting the last ten pounds to America. It was for the support of those whom God had committed to my care, and whom I love as I can no others. I had no friend in London to whom I could apply for temporary aid. My friend, Mr. T——, was out of town, and I did not know his address.

The dark day was rapidly passing away,—the clock in the hall had struck six. I had given up all hopes of reaching Worcester the next day, and had just rung the bell for the servant to bring me some tea, when a gentle tap at the door was heard; the servant entered, and informed me that a gentleman below was wishing to see me. I bade her fetch a light and ask him up. The stranger was my young friend, Frederick Stevenson, son of the excellent minister of the Borough-Road Chapel. I had lectured in this chapel a few days previous; and this young gentleman, with more than ordinary zeal and enthusiasm for the cause of bleeding humanity, and respect for me, had gone amongst his father's congregation and sold a number of copies of my book, and had come to bring me the money. I wiped the silent tear from my eyes as the young man placed the thirteen half-crowns in my hand. I did not let him know under what obligation I was to him for this disinterested act of kindness. He does not know to this day what aid he has rendered to a stranger in a strange land, and I feel that I am but discharging in a trifling degree my debt of gratitude to this young gentleman, in acknowledging my obligation to him. As the man who called for bread and cheese, when feeling in his pocket for the last threepence to pay for it, found a sovereign that he was not aware he possessed, countermanded the order for the lunch, and bade them bring him the best dinner they could get; so I told the servant, when she brought the tea, that I had changed my mind, and should go out to dine. With the means in my pocket of reaching Worcester the next day, I sat down to dinner at the Adelphi, with a good cut of roast beef before me, and felt myself once more at home. Thus ended a dark day in London.

For some days past the sun has not shown his face; clouds have obscured the sky, and the rain has fallen in torrents, which has contributed much to the general gloom. However, I have spent the time in as agreeable a manner as I well could. Yesterday I fulfilled an engagement to dine with a gentleman at the Whittington Club. One who is unacquainted with the club system as carried on in London can scarcely imagine the conveniences they present. Every member appears to be at home, and all seem to own a share in the club. There is a free-and-easy way with those who frequent clubs, and a license given there, that is unknown in the drawing-room of the private mansion. I met the gentleman at the club at the appointed hour, and after his writing my name in the visitors' book, we proceeded to the dining-room, where we partook of a good dinner.

We had been in the room but a short time, when a small man, dressed in black, with his coat buttoned up to the chin, entered the saloon, and took a seat at the table hard by. My friend, in a low whisper, informed me that this person was one of the French refugees. He was apparently not more than thirty years of age, and exceedingly good-looking,— his person being slight, his feet and hands very small and well-shaped, especially his hands, which were covered with kid gloves, so tightly drawn on that the points of the finger-nails were visible through them. His face was mild and almost womanly in its beauty, his eyes soft and full, his brow open and ample, his features well defined, and approaching to the ideal Greek in contour; the lines about his mouth were exquisitely sweet, and yet resolute in expression; his hair was short—his having no moustache gave him nothing of the look of a Frenchman; and I was not a little surprised when informed that the person before me was Louis Blanc. I could scarcely be persuaded to believe that one so small, so child-like in stature, had taken a prominent part in the revolution of 1848. He held in his hand a copy of La Presse, and as soon as he was seated opened it and began to devour its contents. The gentleman with whom I was dining was not acquainted with him, but at the close of our dinner he procured me an introduction through another gentleman.

As we were returning to our lodgings, we saw in Exeter-street, Strand, one of those exhibitions that can be seen in almost any of the streets in the suburbs of the metropolis, but which is something of a novelty to those from the other side of the Atlantic. This was an exhibition of "Punch and Judy." Everything was in full operation when we reached the spot. A puppet appeared, eight or ten inches from the waist upwards, with an enormous face, huge nose, mouth widely grinning, projecting chin, cheeks covered with grog-blossoms, a large protuberance on his back, another on his chest; yet with these deformities he appeared uncommonly happy. This was Mr. Punch. He held in his right hand a tremendous bludgeon, with which he amused himself by rapping on the head every one who came within his reach. This exhibition seems very absurd, yet not less than one hundred were present—children, boys, old men, and even gentlemen and ladies, were standing by, and occasionally greeting the performer with the smile of approbation. Mr. Punch, however, was not to have it all his own way, for another and better sort of Punch-like exhibition appeared a few yards off, that took away Mr. Punch's audience, to the great dissatisfaction of that gentleman. This was an exhibition called the Fantoccini, and far superior to any of the street performances which I have yet seen. The curtain rose and displayed a beautiful theatre in miniature, and most gorgeously painted. The organ which accompanied it struck up a hornpipe, and a sailor, dressed in his blue jacket, made his appearance, and commenced keeping time with the utmost correctness. This figure was not so long as Mr. Punch, but much better looking. At the close of the hornpipe the little sailor made a bow, and tripped off, apparently conscious of having deserved the undivided applause of the bystanders. The curtain dropped; but in two or three minutes it was again up, and a rope was discovered extended on two cross pieces for dancing upon. The tune was changed to an air in which the time was marked; a graceful figure appeared, jumped upon the rope with its balance-pole, and displayed all the manœuvres of an expert performer on the tight-rope. Many who would turn away in disgust from Mr. Punch will stand for hours and look at the performances of the Fantoccini. If people, like the Vicar of Wakefield, will sometimes "allow themselves to be happy," they can hardly fail to have a hearty laugh at the drolleries of the Fantoccini. There may be degrees of absurdity in the manner of wasting our time, but there is an evident affectation in decrying these humble and innocent exhibitions, by those who will sit till two or three in the morning to witness a pantomime at a theatre royal.

An autumn sun shone brightly through a remarkably transparent atmosphere this morning, which was a most striking contrast to the weather we had had during the past three days; and I again set out to see some of the lions of the city, commencing with the Tower of London. Every American, on returning home from a visit to the Old World, speaks with pride of the places he saw while in Europe; and of the many resorts of interest he has read of, few have made a more lasting impression upon his memory than the Tower of London. The stories of the imprisoning of kings and queens, the murdering of princes, the torturing of men and women, without regard to birth, education or station, and of the burning and rebuilding of the old pile, have all sunk deep into his heart. A walk of twenty minutes, after being set down at the bank by an omnibus, brought me to the gate of the Tower. A party of friends who were to meet me there had not arrived; so I had an opportunity of inspecting the grounds, and taking a good view of the external appearance of the old and celebrated building. The Tower is surrounded by a high wall, and around this a deep ditch partly filled with stagnated water. The wall encloses twelve acres of ground, on which stand the several towers, occupying, with their walks and avenues, the whole space. The most ancient part of the building is called the "White Tower," so as to distinguish it from the parts more recently built. Its walls are seventeen feet in thickness, and ninety-two in height, exclusive of the turrets, of which there are four. My company arrived, and we entered the Tower through four massive gates, the innermost one being pointed out as the "Water, or Traitors' Gate," so called from the fact that it opened to the river, and through it the criminals were usually brought to the prison within. But this passage is now closed up. We visited the various apartments in the old building. The room in the Bloody Tower where the infant princes were put to death by the command of their uncle, Richard III., also the recess behind the gate where the bones of the young princes were concealed, were shown to us. The warden of the prison, who showed us through, seemed to have little or no veneration for Henry VIII.; for he often cracked a joke or told a story at the expense of the murderer of Anne Boleyn. The old man wiped the tear from his eye as he pointed out the grave of Lady Jane Grey. This was doubtless one of the best as well as most innocent of those who lost their lives in the Tower; young, virtuous and handsome, she became a victim to the ambition of her own and her husband's relations. I tried to count the names on the wall in "Beauchamp's Tower," but they were too numerous. Anne Boleyn was imprisoned here. The room in the "Brick Tower" where Lady Jane Grey was imprisoned was pointed out as a place of interest. We were next shown into the "White Tower." We passed through a long room filled with many things having a warlike appearance; and among them a number of equestrian figures, as large as life, and clothed in armor and trappings of the various reigns from Edward I. to James II., or from 1272 to 1685. Elizabeth, beth, or the "Maiden Queen," as the warden called her, was the most imposing of the group; she was on a cream-colored charger. We left the Maiden Queen, to examine the cloak upon which General Wolf died at the storming of Quebec. In this room Sir Walter Raleigh was imprisoned, and here was written his "History of the World." In his own hand, upon the wall, is written, "Be thou faithful unto death, and I will give thee a crown of life." His Bible is still shown, with these memorable lines written in it by himself a short time before his death:

> "Even such is Time, that takes on trust,
> Our youth, our joy, our all we have,
> And pays us but with age and dust;
> Who in the dark and silent grave,
> When we have wandered all our ways,
> Shuts up the story of our days."

Spears, battle-axes, pikes, helmets, targets, bows and arrows, and many instruments of torture, whose names I did not learn, grace the walls of this room. The block on which the Earl of Essex and Anne Boleyn were beheaded was shown among other objects of interest. A view of the "Queen's Jewels" closed our visit to the Tower. The gold staff of St. Edward, and the Baptismal Font used at the royal christenings, made of solid silver, and more than four feet high, were among the jewels here exhibited. The Sword of Justice was there, as if to watch the rest of the valuables. However, this was not the sword that Peter used. Our acquaintance with De Foe, Sir Walter Raleigh and Chaucer, through their writings, and the knowledge that they had been incarcerated within the walls of the bastile that we were just leaving, caused us to look back again and again upon its dark-gray turrets.

I closed the day with a look at the interior of St. Paul's Cathedral. A service was just over, and we met a crowd coming out as we entered the great building. "Service is over, and tuppence for all that wants to stay," was the first sound that caught our ears. In the Burlesque of "Esmeralda," a man is met in the belfry of the Notre Dame at Paris, and, being asked for money by one of the vergers, says,

> "I paid three pence at the door,
> And since I came in a great deal more;
> Upon my honor, you have emptied my purse,—
> St. Paul's Cathedral could not do worse."

I felt inclined to join in this sentiment before I left the church. A fine statue of "Surly Sam" Johnson was one of the first things that caught our eyes on looking around. A statue of Sir Edward Packenham, who fell at the battle of New Orleans, was on the opposite side of the great hall. As we had walked over the ground where the general fell, we viewed his statue with more than ordinary interest. We were taken from one scene of interest to another, until we found ourselves in the "Whispering Gallery." From the dome we had a splendid view of the metropolis of the world. A scaffold was erected up here to enable an artist to take sketches, from which a panorama of London was painted. The artist was three years at work. The painting is now exhibited at the Colosseum; but the brain of the artist was turned, and he died insane. Indeed, one can scarcely conceive how it could be otherwise. You in America have no idea of the immensity of this building. Pile together half a dozen of the largest churches in New York or Boston, and you will have but a faint representation of St. Paul's Cathedral.

I have just returned from a stroll of two hours through Westminster Abbey. We entered the building at a door near Poet's Corner, and, naturally enough, looked around for the monuments of the men whose imaginative powers have contributed so much to instruct and amuse mankind. I was not a little disappointed in the few I saw. In almost any church-yard you may see monuments and tombs far superior to anything in Poets' Corner. A few only have monuments. Shakspeare, who wrote of man to man, and for man to the end of time, is honored with one. Addison's monument is also there; but the greater number have nothing more erected to their memories than busts or medallions. Poets' Corner is not splendid in appearance, yet I observed visitors lingering about it, as if they were tied to the spot by love and veneration for some departed friend. All seemed to regard it as classic ground. No sound louder than a whisper was heard during the whole time, except the verger treading over the marble floor with a light step. There is great pleasure in sauntering about the tombs of those with whom we are familiar through their writings; and we tear ourselves from their ashes, as we would from those of a bosom friend. The genius of these men spreads itself over the whole panorama of nature, giving us one vast and varied picture, the color of which will endure to the end of time. None can portray like the poet the passions of the human soul. The statue of Addison, clad in his dressing-gown, is not far from that of Shakspeare. He looks as if he had just left the study, after finishing some chosen paper for the *Spectator*. This memento of a great man was the work of the British public. Such a mark of national respect was but justice to the one who had contributed more to purify and raise the standard of English literature than any man of his day. We next visited the other end of the same transept, near the northern door. Here lie Mansfield, Chatham, Fox, the second William Pitt, Grattan, Wilberforce and a few other statesmen. But, above all, is the stately monument of the Earl of Chatham. In no other place so small do so many great men lie together. To these men, whose graves strangers from all parts of the world wish to view, the British public are in a great measure indebted for England's fame. The high preëminence which England has so long enjoyed and maintained in the scale of empire has constantly been the boast and pride of the English people. The warm panegyrics that have been lavished on her constitution and laws, the songs chanted to celebrate her glory, the lustre of her arms, as the glowing theme of her warriors, the thunder of her artillery in proclaiming her moral prowess, her flag being unfurled to every breeze and ocean, rolling to her shores the tribute of a thousand realms, show England to be the greatest nation in the world, and speak volumes for the great departed, as well as for those of the living present. One requires no company, no amusements, no books, in such a place as this. Time and death have placed within those walls sufficient to occupy the mind, if one should stay here a week.

On my return, I spent an hour very pleasantly in

the Royal Academy, in the same building as the National Gallery. Many of the paintings here are of a fine order. Oliver Cromwell looking upon the headless corpse of King Charles I. appeared to draw the greatest number of spectators. A scene from "As You Like It" was one of the best executed pieces we saw. This was "Rosalind, Celia and Orlando." The artist did himself and the subject great credit. Kemble, in Hamlet, with that ever-memorable skull in his hand, was one of the pieces which we viewed with no little interest. It is strange that Hamlet is always represented as a thin, lean man, when the Hamlet of Shakspeare was a fat, John Bull kind of a man.

[. . .]

In coming out we stopped a short while in the upper room of the gallery, and spent a few minutes over a painting representing Mrs. Siddons in one of Shakspeare's characters. This is by Sir Joshua Reynolds, and is only one of the many pieces that we have seen of this great artist. His genius was vast and powerful in its grasp, his fancy fertile, and his inventive faculty inexhaustible in its resources. He displayed the very highest powers of genius by the thorough originality of his conceptions, and by the entirely new path that he struck out in art. Well may Englishmen be proud of his name. And as time shall step between his day and those that follow after him, the more will his works be appreciated. We have since visited his grave, and stood over his monument in St. Paul's.

Some days since, I left the metropolis to fulfil a few engagements to visit provincial towns; and after a ride of nearly eight hours, we were in sight of the ancient city of York. It was night, the moon was in her zenith, and there seemed nothing between her and the earth but glittering cold. The moon, the stars, and the innumerable gas-lights, gave the city a panoramic appearance. Like a mountain starting out of a plain, there stood the cathedral in its glory, looking down upon the surrounding buildings, with all the appearance of a Gulliver standing over the Lilliputians. Night gave us no opportunity to view the minster. However, we were up the next morning before the sun, and walking round the cathedral with a degree of curiosity seldom excited within us. It is thought that a building of the same dimensions would take fifty years to complete it at the present time, even with all the improvements of the nineteenth century, and would cost no less than the enormous sum of two millions of pounds sterling. From what I had heard of this famous cathedral, my expectations were raised to the highest point; but it surpassed all the idea that I had formed of it. On entering the building, we lost all thought of the external appearance by the matchless beauty of the interior. The echo produced by the tread of our feet upon the floor as we entered, resounding through the aisles, seemed to say, "Put off your shoes, for the place whereon you tread is holy ground." We stood with hat in hand, and gazed with wonder and astonishment down the incomparable vista of more than five hundred feet. The organ, which stands near the centre of the building, is said to be one of the finest in the world. A wall, in front of which is a screen of the most gorgeous and florid architecture, and executed in solid stone, separates the nave from the service choir. The beautiful workmanship of this makes it appear so perfect, as almost to produce the belief that it is tracery-work of wood. We ascended the rough stone steps through a winding stair to the turrets, where we had such a view of the surrounding country as can be obtained from no other place. On the top of the centre and highest turret is a grotesque figure of a fiddler; rather a strange-looking object, we thought, to occupy the most elevated pinnacle on the house of God. All dwellings in the neighborhood appear like so many dwarfs crouching at the feet of the minster; while its own vastness and beauty impress the observer with feelings of awe and sublimity. As we stood upon the top of this stupendous mountain of ecclesiastical architecture, and surveyed the picturesque hills and valleys around, imagination recalled the tumult of the sanguinary battles fought in sight of the edifice. The rebellion of Octavius near three thousand years ago, his defeat and flight to the Scots, his return and triumph over the Romans, and being crowned king of all Britain; the assassination of Oswald, King of the Northumbrians; the flaying alive of Osbert; the crowning of Richard III.; the siege by William the Conqueror; the siege by Cromwell, and the pomp and splendor with which the different monarchs had been received in York, all appeared to be vividly before me. While we were thus calling to our aid our knowledge of history, a sweet peal from the lungs of the ponderous organ below cut short our stay among the turrets, and we descended to have our organ of tune gratified, as well as to finish the inspection of the interior.

I have heard the sublime melodies of Handel, Haydn and Mozart, performed by the most skilful musicians; I have listened with delight and awe to the soul-moving compositions of those masters, as they have been chanted in the most magnificent churches; but never did I hear such music, and played upon such an instrument, as that sent forth by the great organ in the Cathedral of York. The verger took much delight in showing us the horn that was once mounted with gold, but is now garnished with brass. We viewed the monuments and tombs of the departed, and then spent an hour before the great north window. The design on the painted glass, which tradition states was given to the church by five virgin sisters, is the finest thing of the kind in Great Britain. I felt a relief on once more coming into the open air, and again beholding Nature's own sunlight. The splendid ruin of St. Mary's Abbey, with its eight beautiful light Gothic windows, next attracted our attention. A visit to the castle finished our stay in York; and as we were leaving the old city we almost imagined that we heard the chiming of the bells for the celebration of the first Christian Sabbath, with Prince Arthur as the presiding genius.

England stands preeminently the first government in the world for freedom of speech and of the press. Not even in our own beloved America can the man who feels himself oppressed speak as he can in Great Britain. In some parts of England, however, the freedom of thought is tolerated to a greater extent than in others; and of the places favorable to reforms of all kinds, calculated to elevate and benefit mankind, Newcastle-on-Tyne doubtless takes the lead.

Surrounded by innumerable coalmines, it furnishes employment for a large laboring population, many of whom take a deep interest in the passing events of the day, and, consequently, are a reading class. The public debater or speaker, no matter what may be his subject, who fails to get an audience in other towns, is sure of a gathering in the Music Hall, or Lecture Room, in Newcastle.

Here I first had an opportunity of coming in contact with a portion of the laboring people of Britain. I have addressed large and influential meetings in Newcastle and the neighboring towns, and the more I see and learn of the condition of the working-classes of England, the more I am satisfied of the utter fallacy of the statements often made that their condition approximates to that of the slaves of America. Whatever may be the disadvantages that the British peasant labors under, he is free; and if he is not satisfied with his employer, he can make choice of another. He also has the right to educate his children; and he is the equal of the most wealthy person before an English court of justice. But how is it with the American slave? He has no right to himself; no right to protect his wife, his child, or his own person. He is nothing more than a living tool. Beyond his field or workshop he knows nothing. There is no amount of ignorance he is not capable of. He has not the least idea of the face of this earth, nor of the history or constitution of the country in which he dwells. To him the literature, science and art, the progressive history and the accumulated discoveries of by-gone ages, are as if they had never been. The past is to him as yesterday, and the future scarcely more than to-morrow. Ancestral monuments he has none; written documents, fraught with cogitations of other times, he has none; and any instrumentality calculated to awaken and expound the intellectual activity and comprehension of a present or approaching generation, he has none. His condition is that of the leopard of his own native Africa. It lives, it propagates its kind; but never does it indicate a movement towards that all but angelic intelligence of man. The slave eats, drinks and sleeps, all for the benefit of the man who claims his body as his property. Before the tribunals of his country he has no voice. He has no higher appeal than the mere will of his owner. He knows nothing of the inspired Apostles through their writings. He has no Sabbath, no church, no Bible, no means of grace,—and yet we are told that he is as well off as the laboring classes of England. It is not enough that the people of my country should point to their Declaration of Independence, which declares that "all men are created equal." It is not enough that they should laud to the skies a constitution containing boasting declarations in favor of freedom. It is not enough that they should extol the genius of Washington, the patriotism of Henry, or the enthusiasm of Otis. The time has come when nations are judged by the acts of the present, instead of the past. And so it must be with America. In no place in the United Kingdom has the American slave warmer friends than in Newcastle.

I am now in Sheffield, and have just returned from a visit to James Montgomery, the poet. In company with James Wall, Esq., I proceeded to the Mount, the residence of Mr. Montgomery; and our names being sent in, we were soon in the presence of the "Christian poet." He held in his left hand the *Eclectic Review* for the month, and with the right gave me a hearty shake, and bade me "Welcome to Old England." He was anything but like the portraits I had seen of him, and the man I had in my mind's eye. I had just been reading his "Pelican Island," and I eyed the poet with no little interest. He is under the middle size; his forehead high and well formed, the top of which was a little bald; his hair of a yellowish color, his eyes rather small and deep-set, the nose long and slightly acquiline, his mouth rather small, and not at all pretty. He was dressed in black, and a large white cravat entirely hid his neck and chin; his having been afflicted from childhood with salt-rheum was doubtless the cause of his chin being so completely buried in the neckcloth. Upon the whole, he looked more like one of our American Methodist parsons than any one I have seen in this country. He entered freely into conversation with us. He said he should be glad to attend my lecture that evening, but that he had long since quit going out at night. He mentioned having heard William Lloyd Garrison some years before, and with whom he was well pleased. He said it had long been a puzzle to him how Americans could hold slaves and still retain their membership in the churches. When we rose to leave, the old man took my hand between his two, and with tears in his eyes said, "Go on your Christian mission, and may the Lord protect and prosper you! Your enslaved countrymen have my sympathy, and shall have my prayers." Thus ended our visit to the bard of Sheffield.

[. . .]

My last left me under the hospitable roof of Harriet Martineau. I had long had an invitation to visit this distinguished friend of our race, and as the invitation was renewed during my tour through the north, I did not feel disposed to decline it, and thereby lose so favorable an opportunity of meeting with one who had written so much in behalf of the oppressed of our land. About a mile from the head of Lake Windermere, and immediately under Wonsfell, and encircled by mountains on all sides except the south-west, lies the picturesque little town of Ambleside; and the brightest spot in the place is "The Knoll," the residence of Miss Martineau.

We reached "The Knoll" a little after night-fall, and a cordial shake of the hand by Miss M., who was waiting for us, trumpet in hand, soon assured us that we had met with a warm friend.

It is not my intention to lay open the scenes of domestic life at "The Knoll," nor to describe the social parties of which my friends and I were partakers during our sojourn within the hospitable walls of this distinguished writer; but the name of Miss M. is so intimately connected with the Anti-slavery movement by her early writings, and those have been so much admired by the friends of the slave in the United States, that I deem it not at all out of place for me to give my readers some idea of the authoress of "Political Economy," "Travels in the East," "The Hour and the Man," &c.

The dwelling is a cottage of moderate size, built after Miss M.'s own plan, upon a rise of land, from which it derives the name of "The Knoll." The library is the largest room in the building, and upon the walls of it were hung some beautiful engravings and a continental map. On a long table, which occupied the centre of the room, were the busts of Shakspeare, Newton, Milton, and a few other literary characters of the past. One side of the room was taken up with a large case, filled with a choice collection of books; and everything indicated that it was the home of genius and of taste.

The room usually occupied by Miss M., and where we found her on the evening of our arrival, is rather small, and lighted by two large windows. The walls of this room were also decorated with prints and pictures, and on the mantel-shelf were some models in terra cotta of Italian groups. On a circular table lay casts, medallions, and some very choice water-color drawings. Under the south window stood a small table covered with newly-opened letters, a portfolio, and several new books, with here and there a page turned down, and one with a paperknife between its leaves, as if it had only been half read. I took up the last-mentioned, and it proved to be the "Life and Poetry of Hartley Coleridge," son of S. T. Coleridge. It was just from the press, and had, a day or two before, been forwarded to her by the publisher. Miss M. is very deaf, and always carries in her left hand a trumpet; and I was not a little surprised on learning from her that she had never enjoyed the sense of smell, and only on one occasion the sense of taste, and that for a single moment. Miss M. is loved with a sort of idolatry by the people of Ambleside, and especially the poor, to whom she gives a course of lectures every winter gratuitously. She finished her last course the day before our arrival. She was much pleased with Ellen Craft, and appeared delighted with the story of herself and husband's escape from slavery, as related by the latter, during the recital of which I several times saw the silent tear stealing down her cheek, and which she tried in vain to hide from us.

When Craft had finished, she exclaimed, "I would that every woman in the British empire could hear that tale as I have, so that they might know how their own sex was treated in that boasted land of liberty." It seems strange to the people of this country, that one so white and so ladylike as Mrs. Craft should have been a slave, and forced to leave the land of her nativity and seek an asylum in a foreign country.

[. . .]

After remaining a short time, and reading the epitaphs of the departed, we again returned to "The Knoll." Nothing can be more imposing than the beauty of English park scenery, and especially in the vicinity of the Lakes. Magnificent lawns that extend like sheets of vivid green, with here and there a sprinkling of fine trees, heaping up rich piles of foliage, and then the forest with the hare, the deer, and the rabbit, "bounding away to the covert, or the pheasant suddenly bursting upon the wing—the artificial stream, the brook taught to wind in natural meanderings, or expand into the glassy lake, with the yellow leaf sleeping upon its bright waters, and occasionally a rustic temple or sylvan statue grown green and dark with age," give an air of sanctity and picturesque beauty to English scenery that is unknown in the United States. The very laborer with his thatched cottage and narrow slip of ground-plot before the door, the little flower-bed, the woodbine trimmed against the wall, and hanging its blossoms about the windows, and the peasant seen trudging home at nightfall with the avails of the toil of the day upon his back—all this tells us of the happiness both of rich and poor in this country. And yet there are those who would have the world believe that the laborer of England is in a far worse condition than the slaves of America. Such persons know nothing of the real condition of the working classes of this country. At any rate, the poor here, as well as the rich, are upon a level, as far as the laws of the country are concerned. The more one becomes acquainted with the English people, the more one has to admire them. They are so different from the people of our own country. Hospitality, frankness and good humor, are always to be found in an Englishman. After a ramble of three days about the Lakes, we mounted the coach, bidding Miss Martineau farewell, and quitted the lake district.

Presuming that you will expect from me some account of the great World's Fair, I take my pen to give you my own impressions, although I am afraid that anything which I may say about this "lion of the day" will fall far short of a description. On Monday last, I quitted my lodgings at an early hour, and started for the Crystal Palace. The day was fine, such as we seldom experience in London, with a clear sky, and invigorating air, whose vitality was as rousing to the spirits as a blast from the "horn of Astolpho." Although it was not yet ten o'clock when I entered Piccadilly, every omnibus was full, inside and out, and the street was lined with one living stream, as far as the eye could reach, all wending their way to the "Glass House." No metropolis in the world presents such facilities as London for the reception of the Great Exhibition now collected within its walls. Throughout its myriads of veins the stream of industry and toil pulses with sleepless energy. Every one seems to feel that this great capital of the world is the fittest place wherein they might offer homage to the dignity of toil. I had already begun to feel fatigued by my pedestrian excursions as I passed "Apsley House," the residence of the Duke of Wellington, and emerged into Hyde Park.

I had hoped that on getting into the Park I would be out of the crowd that seemed to press so heavily in the street. But in this I was mistaken. I here found myself surrounded by and moving with an overwhelming mass, such as I had never before witnessed. And, away in the distance, I beheld a dense crowd, and above every other object was seen the lofty summit of the Crystal Palace. The drive in the Park was lined with princely-looking vehicles of every description. The drivers in their bright red and gold uniforms, the pages and footmen in their blue trousers and white silk stockings, and the horses dressed up in their neat, silver-mounted harness, made the scene altogether one of great splendor. I was soon at the door, paid my shilling, and entered the building at the south end of the transept. For the first ten or twenty minutes, I was so lost in astonishment, and absorbed in pleasing wonder, that I could do nothing but gaze up and down the vista of the noble building. The Crystal Palace resembles in some respects the interior of the cathedrals of this country. One long avenue from east to west is intercepted by a transept, which divides the building into two nearly equal parts. This is the greatest building the world ever saw, before which the Pyramids of Egypt, and the Colossus of Rhodes must hide their diminished heads. The palace was not full at any time during the day, there being only sixty-four thousand persons present. Those who love to study the human countenance in all its infinite varieties can find ample scope for the indulgence of their taste, by a visit to the World's Fair. All countries are there represented—Europeans, Asiatics, Americans and Africans, with their numerous subdivisions. Even the exclusive Chinese, with his hair braided, and hanging down his back, has left the land of his nativity, and is seen making long strides through the Crystal Palace, in his wooden-bottomed shoes. Of all places of curious costumes and different fashions, none has ever yet presented such a variety as this Exhibition. No dress is too absurd to be worn in this place.

There is a great deal of freedom in the Exhibition. The servant who walks behind his mistress through the Park feels that he can crowd against her in the Exhibition. The queen and the day laborer, the prince and the merchant, the peer and the pauper, the Celt and the Saxon, the Greek and the Frank, the Hebrew and the Russ, all meet here upon terms of perfect equality. This amalgamation of rank, this kindly blending of interests, and forgetfulness of the cold formalities of ranks and grades, cannot but be attended with the very best results. I was pleased to see such a goodly sprinkling of my own countrymen in the Exhibition—I mean colored men and women—well-dressed, and moving about with their fairer brethren. This, some of our proslavery Americans did not seem to relish very well. There was no help for it. As I walked through the American part of the Crystal Palace some of our Virginia neighbors eyed me closely and with jealous looks, especially as an English lady was leaning on my arm. But their sneering looks did not disturb me in the least. I remained the longer in their department, and criticized the bad appearance of their goods the more. Indeed, the Americans, as far as appearance goes, are behind every other country in the Exhibition. The "Greek Slave" is the only production of art which the United States has sent. And it would have been more to their credit had they kept that at home. In so vast a place as the Great Exhibition one scarcely knows what to visit first, or what to look upon last. After wandering about through the building for five hours, I sat down in one of the galleries and looked at the fine marble statue of Virginius, with the knife in his hand and about to take the life of his beloved and beautiful daughter, to save her from the hands of Appius Claudius. The admirer of genius will linger for hours among the great variety of statues in the long avenue. Large statues of Lords Eldon and Stowell, carved out of solid marble, each weighing above twenty tons, are among the most gigantic in the building.

I was sitting with my four hundred paged guide-book before me, and looking down upon the moving mass, when my attention was called to a small group of gentlemen standing near the statue of Shake-speare, one of whom wore a white coat and hat, and had flaxen hair, and trousers rather short in the legs. The lady by my side, and who had called my atten-tion to the group, asked if I could tell what country this odd-looking gentleman was from. Not wishing to run the risk of a mistake, I was about declining to venture an opinion, when the reflection of the sun against a mirror, on the opposite side, threw a bril-liant light upon the group, and especially on the face of the gentleman in the white coat, and I immedi-ately recognized under the brim of the white hat the features of Horace Greeley, Esq., of the New York *Tribune*. His general appearance was as much out of the English style as that of the Turk whom I had seen but a moment before, in his bag-like trou-sers, shuffling along in his slippers. But oddness in dress is one of the characteristics of the Great Exhibition.

Among the many things in the Crystal Palace, there are some which receive greater attention than others, around which may always be seen large groups of the visitors. The first of these is the Koh-i-noor, the "Mountain of Light." This is the largest and most valuable diamond in the world, said to be worth two million pounds sterling. It is indeed a great source of attraction to those who go to the Exhibition for the first time, but it is doubtful whether it obtains such admiration afterwards. We saw more than one spectator turn away with the idea that, after all, it was only a piece of glass. After some jamming, I got a look at the precious jewel; and although in a brass-grated cage, strong enough to hold a lion, I found it to be no larger than the third of a hen's egg. Two policemen remain by its side day and night.

The finest thing in the Exhibition is the "Veiled Vestal," a statue of a woman carved in marble, with a veil over her face, and so neatly done that it looks as if it had been thrown over after it was finished. The Exhibition presents many things which appeal to the eye and touch the heart, and altogether it is so decorated and furnished as to excite the dullest mind, and satisfy the most fastidious.

England has contributed the most useful and substantial articles; France, the most beautiful; while Russia, Turkey and the West Indies, seem to vie with each other in richness. China and Persia are not behind. Austria has also contributed a rich and beautiful stock. Sweden, Norway, Denmark, and the smaller states of Europe, have all tried to outdo themselves in sending goods to the World's Fair. In machinery, England has no competitor. In art, France is almost alone in the Exhibition, setting aside England.

In natural productions and provisions, America stands alone in her glory. There lies her pile of canvassed hams; whether they were wood or real, we could not tell. There are her barrels of salt beef and pork, her beautiful white lard, her Indian-corn and corn-meal, her rice and tobacco, her beef-tongues, dried peas, and a few bags of cotton. The contributors from the United States seemed to have forgotten that this was an exhibition of art, or they most certainly would not have sent provisions. But the United States takes the lead in the contributions, as no other country has sent in provisions. The finest thing contributed by our countrymen is a large piece of silk with an eagle painted upon it, surrounded by stars and stripes.

After remaining more than five hours in the great

temple, I turned my back upon the richly-laden stalls, and left the Crystal Palace. On my return home I was more fortunate than in the morning, inasmuch as I found a seat for my friend and myself in an omnibus. And even my ride in the close omnibus was not without interest. For I had scarcely taken my seat, when my friend, who was seated opposite me, with looks and gesture informed me that we were in the presence of some distinguished person. I eyed the countenances of the different persons, but in vain, to see if I could find any one who by his appearance showed signs of superiority over his fellow-passengers. I had given up the hope of selecting the person of note, when another look from my friend directed my attention to a gentleman seated in the corner of the omnibus. He was a tall man, with strongly-marked features, hair dark and coarse. There was a slight stoop of the shoulder— that bend which is almost always a characteristic of studious men. But he wore upon his countenance a forbidding and disdainful frown, that seemed to tell one that he thought himself better than those about him. His dress did not indicate a man of high rank; and had we been in America, I would have taken him for an Ohio farmer.

While I was scanning the features and general appearance of the gentleman, the omnibus stopped and put down three or four of the passengers, which gave me an opportunity of getting a seat by the side of my friend, who, in a low whisper, informed me that the gentleman whom I had been eying so closely was no less a person than Thomas Carlyle. I had read his "Hero-worship," and "Past and Present," and had formed a high opinion of his literary abilities. But his recent attack upon the emancipated people of the West Indies, and his laborious article in favor of the reëstablishment of the lash and slavery, had created in my mind a dislike for the man, and I almost regretted that we were in the same omnibus. In some things Mr. Carlyle is right: but in many he is entirely wrong. As a writer, Mr. Carlyle is often monotonous and extravagant. He does not exhibit a new view of nature, or raise insignificant objects into importance; but generally takes commonplace thoughts and events, and tries to express them in stronger and statelier language than others. He holds no communion with his kind, but stands alone, without mate or fellow. He is like a solitary peak, all access to which is cut off. He exists not by sympathy, but by antipathy. Mr. Carlyle seems chiefly to try how he shall display his own powers, and astonish mankind, by starting new trains of speculation, or by expressing old ones so as not to be understood. He cares little what he says, so as he can say it differently from others. To read his works, is one thing; to understand them, is another. If any one thinks that I exaggerate, let him sit for an hour over "Sartor Resartus," and if he does not rise from its pages, place his three or four dictionaries on the shelf, and say I am right, I promise never again to say a word against Thomas Carlyle. He writes one page in favor of reform, and ten against it. He would hang all prisoners to get rid of them; yet the inmates of the prisons and "workhouses are better off than the poor." His heart is with the poor; yet the blacks of the West Indies should be taught that if they will not raise sugar and cotton by their own free will, "Quashy should have the whip applied to him." He frowns upon the reformatory speakers upon the boards of Exeter Hall; yet he is the prince of reformers. He hates heroes and assassins; yet Cromwell was an angel, and Charlotte Corday a saint. He scorns everything, and seems to be tired of what he is by nature, and tries to be what he is not.

Published 1852

A. B. C. MERRIMAN-LABOR

Augustus Merriman-Labor (1877–1919) was born in Freetown, Sierra Leone. He worked as a clerk for the colonial authorities whilst also developing his literary career by writing. Amongst other work, he wrote a novella and, in 1898, an anonymous exposé of Britain's Hut Tax War against the people of Sierra Leone. In 1904 he travelled to London where he worked as a clerk, taught Sunday school in South London and trained as a barrister at Lincoln's Inn. He also continued with his writing and published his most famous satirical work, *Britons Through Negro Spectacles*, to dispel illusions that other Africans might have about Britain. The book was not a commercial success, and other business failures led to bankruptcy and disbarment. Merriman-Labor was later a munitions worker at the Woolwich Arsenal and died of tuberculosis in Lambeth Workhouse. The following extracts demonstrate the satirical style of his writing about some of his experiences in London.

Britons Through Negro Spectacles

The House of Commons is now considering the proposed new Constitution for Disunited West Africa. Questions are being asked the Secretary of State for the Colonies respecting certain matters affecting the natives under the Constitution in contemplation.

The first questioner is Sir Charles Goodman, on whom evidently the mantle of Wilberforce has fallen. He asks, "How is it that notwithstanding one hundred and twenty years of British rule and civilisation in parts of West Africa, the natives are not considered fit to have a representative government?"

Another Commoner, Mr. James Justice, a member of the Society of Friends—who "were the first to lay a petition on the evils of the slave trade on the table of the House of Commons," and that was in 1783—would like to know why a male suffrage clause in favour of the natives, if not a female one as well, should not be added in the proposed Constitution.

Mr. Harry Hardbone, representing an Irish constituency—remembering it was only after the Union in 1801 between Great Britain and Ireland that the first Parliamentary majority against Negro

145

slavery was secured—is anxious to know why the natives cannot be allowed to rule themselves. The Blacks are to have "home rule," he declares. It is time, he thinks, that England in respect of Africa, should "hands off." He says pointedly: "Any imperialism which does not take cognisance of the claims and rights of the black and yellow races, is selfish racialism, yea less—it is foolish nationalism."

Mr. Carr Harding, a Labour member, sees behind the present attitude of the Government towards the natives, what he describes as "the octopus hands of the grabbing financier squeezing the life-blood of the poor and sweated Africans."

After his remarks, a petition is placed on the table of the House, signed by the Church Missionary Society, the Society for the Propagation of the Gospel in Foreign Parts, the Wesleyan Missionary Society, and other societies which have spent millions of money to educate the natives. This petition prays that the future policy of the Colonial Governments shall differentiate between educated natives and non-educated ones. The signatories think that the present policy is hurtful to the natural pride of the educated native—one who can read and write, or who, perhaps, has received a college or university education here or abroad, or who is a member of some learned profession, since, by such faulty policy, such educated native is classed with an uncivilised one, simply because the colour of their skins is the same.

Another petition is also read, emanating from the Anti-Slavery Society, the Aborigines' Protection Society, the League of Universal Brotherhood, and a number of kindred institutions. In this second petition it is prayed, on the assumption that Whites and Blacks are equal, that the educated natives shall receive under the Colonial Governments and in the Colonial Civil Service, the same advantages as the Whites in regard to position or promotion. They opine that merit alone, and not colour, shall be the consideration for Colonial appointments. It is wrong, according to a case they quote, to appoint as Supreme Judge of Sierra Nigeria, at a thousand pounds a year, Egbert Englishmann who was last among successful examinees for the English Bar, whilst Professor Neil Negroman, Master of Laws, who passed the identical Bar examination with distinction, is merely appointed Chief Clerk in the Crown Law Office of the same Colony at the low annual salary of three hundred pounds. Such and similar wrongs to the natives, the petitioners think ought to receive their death-blow by the proposed new Constitution for Disunited West Africa now under consideration of this meeting of Commons.

To this and the other petitions and to the several questions asked, the Secretary of State for the Colonies merely replies in one brief sentence, a laconigram which for clearness, I am to enlarge in the following statement. He promises to advise His Majesty's Government to send out to West Africa at an early date, at least before anything definite is done, a Commission to collect evidence respecting, and to report on the advisability or otherwise of granting representative government to the natives.

Left to the Secretary of State alone, a Minister who has been reported to be sympathetic towards the natives, matters may be righted. Apart from his own wish on the subject, he has to get the collective opinion and advice of other Ministers. The Ministers would never advise contrary to what they think is the desire of Parliament, or of the more powerful body—the electors of great Britain. But Parliament, as a whole, is not concerned with West Africa, nor have the general electors any desire, or even any mind, on the subject of the natives. The mind of the average elector in Britain as regards West Africa is a perfect blank. He does not even know in what part of the world West Africa is. Besides, he is too busy with his own troubles to think about those of Negroes. We should therefore not expect him to express a desire one way or the other in respect of

British Africans abroad. He is not concerned. The Crown Ministers know this too well. For this and other reasons, they will therefore guide themselves not by what is the probable wish of the general electors, but by what is . . . .

Africanus, I should not say more. I should not spoil your already pleasant visit by referring lengthily to the peace-disturbing subject of peace-seeking politics. For the present, let me say that I do not believe in any Commission such as the one the Secretary of State promises to send out to West Africa. Several have gone out before. With what result? We know best.

WHEN BLACKS MEET WHITES

This want of relish for the colour of the Negro or ignorance about him and his colour, is more evidenced in the words oractions of the common people of the low class suburbs in Britain, by the actions of some thoughtless people of the better class, and amongst children of every class. A story or two will make this clear.

The present Alake of Abeokuta during his recent visit here, was so much annoyed by some thoughtless students of a certain British university, that prompt action was taken by the university authorities to punish the offenders.

As regards the treatment by white children to black people, an anecdote about a Negro bishop first suggests itself to my mind. The late Bishop Crowther was once spending some time in England with a white clergyman, an evangelical missionary who had been out to West Africa. The black prelate was provided with a bed on which was a white sheet. Every morning the clergyman's little daughter would examine the sheet carefully to see whether some of the blackness of the good bishop was left on it.

This puts me in mind of a story I read not long ago in an English weekly magazine respecting a little fellow who returned home from school with his copy book covered all over with what seemed to be splashes of black ink. Asked by his father to explain the filthy condition of his book, the school boy replied that the splashes were caused by a Negro lad who, accidentally cutting his finger, used the copy book to wipe off his black blood.

The other story relates to my humble self. I was once spending a day with a respectable family at Stockwell in South London. The mother introduced me to her little daughter as a person who had come from Africa. The little child looked attentively at me for a while, and then turning to her mother, asked, "Mama! mama! is the African gentleman black all over his body, or only in his hands and face?" The mother replied "Well Mary, I have never seen his body, but I daresay it is black as well."

Little Mary, being a child who had been properly trained, did not bother to use her tongue and spittle on my hand to see if the blackness will come off. A queer white lady did use her spittle on a great-aunt of mine who was brought to England over sixty years ago.

As I speak of my late aunt, I call to mind a tragical story connected with her stay in the white man's country. Her mistress called with her to see a lady in the Midlands, a country woman who had never seen a Negro before. She was not told beforehand that she was to expect a Negro of the she-kind. In consequence, the country lady was so frightened on seeing my aunt suddenly, that, as she opened the door to her and her mistress, with one hand to the handle, she fell down dead.

Whilst this lady had a mortal dread for my aunt, both of them now far away, another lady, an elderly one, once a resident at delightful Dulwich in Southeast London, was extremely fond of me. She wanted me always to visit her because, as she said, people with black hair, and black men more so, always brought her luck. On New Year's Eve, a few years ago, she asked me to call on her at twelve o'clock midnight, so that if I were her very first visitor, she would get luck during the whole year. I called on her as she desired. Strange to say, the year was a very lucky one to her. She became entirely free from her life-long rheumatism. Entirely free,—in fact, more than free, for the painful malady took her to a place where "there shall be no more death, neither sorrow, nor crying, neither shall there be any more pain, for the former things are passed away." She has now ceased to suffer. She is gone.

I am still here, suffering from some people's dislike of my colour, especially when I visit a low class suburb in Britain.

In the low class suburbs a black man stands the chance of being laughed at to scorn until he takes to his heels. And, in such low quarters, until the Diamond Jubilee of the late Queen Victoria which by bringing hundreds of black soldiers and others into Britain made black faces somewhat familar, bad boys will not hesitate to shower stones or rotten eggs on any passing black man, however high he may be in his own estimation.

Pray that, even now, you never meet a troupe of children just from school. They will call you all kinds of names, sing you all sorts of songs, whilst following you about until a passing vehicle flies you out of their sight.

Pray also that you never encounter a band of

factory girls just from their workshop. Some of these girls will make fun of you by throwing kisses to you when not making hisses at you, whilst others shout "Go wash your face guv'nor," or sometimes call out "nigger! nigger! nigger!"

This objectionable epithet recalls a funny experience I had once. I was standing with two other Africans at a corner near Chancery Lane. A poor sickly-looking man turned up and asked alms of us. We could then and there have placed him in charge of a policeman because, as I told you, it is not lawful to beg in England. But this beggar's condition was so apparently pitiable, that we raised about sixpence among ourselves, and gave it to the poor fellow. No sooner had he gone ten yards from us than he shouted, at the same time, taking to his heels, "Nigger, nigger, show me your tail, your coal-black tail."

From the incidents which I have just related, you will see that the people's notion of black men is very limited, and even the limited very vague. A good many Britons believe that all Africans and even Indians in Britain, are from the same country, that they speak the same language, and are known to one another.

Of the black man's country, at least of West Africa, their knowledge is worse still. Apart from the statement that "Sierra Leone is the white man's grave"—a wrong statement indeed—few know anything of any other country in West Africa. Many fancy that the Colony of the Gold Coast is a part of the gold district of Australia. Even their learned men find it difficult to distinguish between Bathurst in New South Wales and Bathurst on the Gambia. The editor of a leading London newspaper could see no difference between Lagos in Southern Nigeria and Lagos in Portugal. Between Liberia in West Africa and Siberia in Russia is a distance of several thousand miles; but not a few believe that the former country is the same as the latter. Not a few believe, as the beggar thought, that inside the trousers of every Negro is a tail like that of a horse.

Published 1909

PETER STANFORD

Rev Peter Thomas Stanford (1858–1909) was born into slavery in Virginia, USA. Orphaned as a child, he temporarily lived both with Native Americans and an adoptive White American family before running away to New York as a teenager. Initially self-taught, he later graduated from a training college and became a Baptist minister in Connecticut and Canada, as well as an abolitionist. He travelled to Britain in 1883 to raise money for his struggling Canadian church. In Britain he married, and in 1889 became the first African American minister in Birmingham when he was appointed pastor of the Hope Street Chapel. In Britain he became known as 'Birmingham's coloured preacher' and was connected with the Society for the Recognition of the Brotherhood of Man. He returned to live in the USA in 1895. In the following extract, he relates some of his experiences in London, Yorkshire and Birmingham.

From Bondage to Liberty

CHAPTER XI.

I REACH ENGLAND—A PENNILESS STRANGER.

I arrived in Liverpool February 14th, 1883, and as I had been robbed during the voyage of what little money I possessed at starting, I found myself penniless on landing. I possessed letters of introduction from friends in Canada to friends in Liverpool, among the number being one from the Secretary of the Young Men's Christian Association in London, Ontario, Canada, to the Secretary of the Y.M.C.A. of Liverpool, and my first effort was devoted to finding that gentleman. As I wended my way through the streets of this great shipping port, how strange and novel everything appeared to me! And what a strange and extraordinary appearance I must have presented to those who observed me! Dressed in the costume of the country I had just left, in long fur top-coat and fur cap, and my feet and legs encased in long Wellington top-boots, I soon became the centre of attraction of a large crowd, whose attention was first called to me by a number of factory girls, one of whom shouted—"Hi! there goes Buffalo Bill." The opportune arrival of a policeman on the scene dispersed the crowd, and rescued me from a very embarrassing position, and permitted me to resume my way. I had not proceeded far before I observed what appeared to me a copper coin lying in the gutter, and having picked it up, I was desirous of ascertaining its value, and for this purpose I accosted a gentleman in the street. He eyed me inquisitively, and then said, "I perceive you are a stranger here." He further enquired whence I had come, and my destination. He very kindly proffered to show me the building of which I was in search, and there taking out his watch he enquired, "Have you dined yet?" I replied in the negative, and he invited me to accompany him to a neighbouring restaurant and have lunch with him. During the meal I explained my wishes to him, and when it was ended, he accompanied me to the Y.M.C.A., the Secretary of which, however, was out. I showed the gentleman the letters of introduction I had received for London, and he advised me, as he said it was the great centre of England, to go there at once. He assured me that I ought to begin there, and that I should do better than if I remained in Liverpool; and so to London I resolved to go, and go at once, the sovereign (for such it proved to be) I had picked up in the gutter supplying me with the necessary funds for the fare. Having looked for the time a train would leave, he accompanied me to the station, and had my luggage labelled for London. He could not obtain a ticket, as we were so early they had not commenced the issue of tickets for the train by which I was to leave, so he advised me to take a stroll for about an hour and then return in time for the train, and with that he bade me good-bye. Once more alone, I wandered through the streets looking into the shop windows, and, in thought, selecting various articles I should like to take back home with me. I was very much attracted by a donkey which I saw in a cart in the street, as we have not many in America of the kind they are in England. I had received some idea of the value of money from the gentleman who had just left me, and who had acted so generously towards me. I accosted the possessor of the donkey, and wanted to know the value of such an animal as he was driving. After staring at me, he laughingly offered to sell me the donkey for a pound, and the cart for two pounds, which gave me an idea of the small value of horses and donkeys in this country. I took the man's address, bade him good-day, and turned for the station, or depöt as we call them in my country; but for the life of me I could not find it, and in my dilemma I enquired of a respectable looking man the road to the London depöt, and he took me to a large shop where they sold milk, and which was known as the London and Liverpool depöt; and before I had recovered sufficiently from my surprise to explain or ask further questions, the man had disappeared. A policeman, however, directed me to the station, where I arrived just in time to hear the guard's whistle to start what I believed was my train, and I made a rush to get into a carriage, when I received a lesson in English railway arrangements; for someone seized me, and flung me with such force from the train, that I went spinning across the platform till I came in violent contact with the building, and fell almost senseless against the wall. When I had sufficiently recovered, the danger and folly of my action were pointed out to me, for which I apologised, and explained that I was an entire stranger to the country, its laws and customs. If I had succeeded in entering the train, it afterwards appeared, I should have gone wrong, as it was not the London train. Eventually I was put right, and very shortly was steaming for the town in which I expected to do so much. I arrived in London about ten o'clock the same night, and by the advice of a gentleman who happened to be in the same compartment, put up at the Aldersgate Street Hotel. I was somewhat taken aback by the grandeur of the place, but not knowing what else to do I entered, ordered a room, and, after partaking of some light refreshment, retired for the night. The next morning, without any breakfast, I

159

went out to make a few calls. My first call was upon the Rev. C. H. Spurgeon, but he was too busy to see me. I then went to the Mission House to see Mr. Bayaes, and he could not understand what I wanted, or what I wished to do. During that day I called on several others, but all to no purpose, and in the evening I returned to the hotel, tired, hungry, sick at heart, and, without money, dared not ask for a meal. Remembering I had a few ship biscuits in my box, I went to my bedroom, ate them, then after a good cry, went to sleep; and thus ended my first day's experience in the great city from which I expected such great things. The next morning I called on the Rev. W. T. More, M.A., L.L.D., editor of the *Christian Commonwealth*, but as he was not in, I saw the Rev. G. Brooke, one of the staff of the paper, who asked me to take an evening service at his church; but he did not fix the date then, which was arranged some time after. I afterwards called upon the Secretary of the Young Men's Christian Association, Exeter Hall, and from there I went to the Y.M.C.A. in Aldersgate Street, from whom I received some good advice; and when he ascertained where I was staying, he told me that I had better leave at once, and lent me money to pay the expenses I had already incurred. I followed the advise he gave me immediately, and obtained lodgings with a private family. The next day I again sought an interview with the Rev. W. T. More, at the office of the *Christian Commonwealth*. He received me very kindly, and gave me the following letter:-

Editorial Department, The Christian
   Commonwealth,
Kensington Chambers, 73, Ludgate Hill,
   London, E.C., April 2nd, 1883.

Having a full knowledge of the condition of the coloured people in Canada, we feel sure that the plea of the Rev. P. T. Stanford, of London. Canada, is worthy of the sympathy of all Christians in this country. Mr. P. T. Stanford's credentials are, to us, entirely satisfactory.

REV. W. T. MOORE, REV. G. BROOKE.

By his advice I called on Messrs. Morgan and Scott, editors of *The Christian*, and they also received me kindly. Altogether, I spent about two months wandering the streets of London, and for the greater portion of the time without sufficient or proper food, and in constant dread of being ejected from my lodgings. During this time I met a few coloured men, whose pursuits, however, were of a questionable character—hangers on at low theatres, dancers at cheap concert halls, and the like. One or two I met had some slight acquaintance with me before they left America, and from them I received an occasional meal. They also offered to obtain employment for me with themselves, for try as I would, I could not succeed in obtaining work for myself. Two of these would-be friends called on me one day, and offered me employment of the character just mentioned, telling me at the same time that they could earn from twenty to thirty shillings per week. I confess it was a great temptation, for I had been two days with nothing but a loaf of bread upon which to subsist, and where the next loaf was to come from I had not the least idea. They endeavoured to show me the folly of my ways by pointing out the uselessness of my trying to become or keep up the appearance of a person in such a country as England, and expressed a most decided opinion that my Christianity would never obtain me a livelihood. They left me for about an hour to consider the matter over, whilst they transacted some other business, when said they would call again for a decisive answer. A few minutes after their departure I was on my knees, earnestly praying God to assist me, when I was interrupted by a knock at the door from my landlady, who handed me the Revd. George Brooks' letter:—(see Appendix A). I read this letter over and over again to make sure of its import, and at length, being satisfied with the meaning, I attended the meeting and delivered an address, at the conclusion of which the deacons gave me £2. My first business the following morning was to pay the rent of my room. My coloured friends called according to their promise, but I did not, neither did I want, to see them; for I felt, notwithstanding their proffered assistance, that in accompanying them I should certainly be journeying the wrong road. The Rev. Mr. Baxter, editor of the *Christian Herald*, found me employment as evangelist, and I remained with him five months, during which time I was enabled to repay the loan received from the Secretary of Aldersgate Street. After concluding my engagement with the Rev. Mr. Baxter, I left London and went to Leeds, Barnsley, and Keighley, in Yorkshire. I found a dear friend in the Rev. John Gregory, minister of the Oak Road Congregational Church, who not only allowed me the use of his schoolroom for my lectures, but permitted me also to retain the proceeds.

June, 1885.

I have been much interested in reading the "Cry of Ex-Slaves," by the Rev. P. T. Stanford, and have much pleasure in commending the book to the public. Mr. Stanford has lectured in the Oak Road Schoolroom, to a highly appreciative audience. I cordially wish him success in his mission.

JOHN GREGORY,
Minister of Oak Road Congregational
Church, Leeds.
Endorsed by H. W. Pech, London and
Yorkshire Bank, Morley.

One day I met a gentleman in the street, who, when in Canada, was one of the teachers in my Sunday school. He had returned home, and was then living in Barnsley, but happened to be on a visit to Leeds. On his invitation, I visited him at his home two or three weeks after our meeting, and while staying with him arrangements were entered into for me to lecture in the town at some future date. I then went to live at Keighley, and through the kindness of the Rev. W. E. Goodman, Pastor of the Albert Street Baptist Chapel, the following services were conducted:—

IN PROFOUND REVERENCE AND VENERATION, IN MEMORY OF OUR MUCH REGRETTED FRIEND, F, BUTTERFIELD, ESQ.—The Mayor of Keighley presided on Monday evening at a meeting in Albert

Street Chapel, Keighley, to hear a lecture by the Rev. P. T. Stanford, a coloured preacher, from Canada. In introducing the Lecturer, the Mayor said they met that evening under the feeling of a deep sorrow. The sad intelligence of Mr. Fred Butterfield's death was in all their minds. It was true that he had spent so many years in America that he seemed to be almost more intimately connected with the United States than with Yorkshire; but of late Mr. Fred Butterfield had been more amongst them, and be knew from them by so great a distance, and having had his home so long in another land, his interest in England, and especially his affection for Keighley, had never diminished. The deceased gentleman told him only recently that during all the years he had been in America, the first paper he opened and the one he read most carefully was that which came from Keighley; and he also said that, although he had seen much that was beautiful in America and on the Continent of Europe, no place had such a charm for him as the place of his birth. In Keighley he was born, and it was his earnest wish that he might be permitted to die there. That wish, however, had not been fulfilled, for the hand of death overtook him near Vichy, where he had gone to drink the waters after spending the winter at Nice. There was a peculiar appropriateness in mentioning Mr. Butterfield's name in connection with the object of that evening's meeting, for he had always been a firm and avowed friend of the slave, when such sentiments were neither popular nor even safe to utter in many parts of America. He was a generous benefactor to all in distress, and was ever ready to assist his fellow townsmen on their arrival in the States. Although nothing that they could do or say would be of any avail, still perhaps it might be some slight comfort to his sorrowing relatives to know that he who had passed away had not fallen unnoticed, that his death was not a mere private grief but a heavy public loss, and that their heartfelt sympathy went out to his mourning relatives.—The Rev. W. E. Goodman, pastor of the Albert Street Chapel, moved a vote of condolence with Mr. Henry, Mrs. F., and Miss Butterfield on their bereavement, and this being seconded by the Rev. P. T. Stanford, of Canada (the lecturer), was carried.—*Keighley News*, June 30th 1883.

CHAPTER XII.
I AM "PERSECUTED BUT NOT FORSAKEN."

In the latter part of 1885, I went to live at Bradford, in Yorkshire. Here I was met with an amount of ill-feeling and mistrust which seemed incredible, but which, I believe, was in a great measure due to the past misconduct of a number of coloured men, and the bad impression they had left behind them. Everybody avoided me, or regarded me askance; even Christian ministers of my own faith, to whom I looked for some kindness and assistance, referred me to Mr. Spurgeon. I had written to that gentleman, but, from some unfortunate misrepresentation, he declined to interest himself in my behalf, his last communication to me reading something like the following:

> From information received respecting you, I have decided not to have anything to do with you. My advice to you is, go to work; you are as able to work as I am.
>
> Yours,
>
> C. H. SPURGEON.

I mentioned this to several, but they expressed their belief also that I was simply an imposter like many other negroes who had preceded me in Bradford. Some of them even went so far as to visit my house and demand my credentials, taking the addresses of several persons from whom I had received letters, and then writing to them for information. It was three weary months after this that I ascertained that letters had been received in Bradford. One of the most officious intermeddlers advised me to leave the town; for, said he, it would be a bad thing for you if the reports are not good. My reply to this piece of advice and expression of his opinion was a demand for the publication of the letters which had been received from America, and which had been in their possession more than a month; and to still further enlighten him I told him that, as I had nothing to fear, I should not budge an inch. I had received letters myself from some of the persons with whom they had been in communication. Through the influence of the Rev. George Edmonson, pastor of the Ripley Street Baptist Chapel, Bradford, a public meeting was called, of which the following is a report:

MISSION TO THE EX. SLAVES NOW IN CANADA.—A meeting was held in Bradford last week, by a committee of gentlemen appointed to inqure into the particulars of the above mission, and also as to whether the Rev. P. T. Stanford was authorised by the church in Canada to collect donations for the better education of ex-slaves in Canada. Mr. Tetley, of Bradford, read letters which had been received from Mr. Macdonald, of Macdonald and Ivey, Barristers, London, Ontario; Rev. A. Telfer, of Barnstaple; Professor H. Smith, of the Connecticut

Literary Institute, where Mr. Stanford matriculated; and Mr. John Pope, one of the deacons of the Baptist Chapel in Canada, with which Mr. Stanford was associated, all confirming the authenticity of the work upon which Mr. Stanford is engaged. After letters were read, the Committee passed the following resolution:—"That this Committee, after hearing the communications received by the deputation appointed as the last committee meeting respecting the Rev. P. T. Stanford's mission to this country, declares itself satisfied with the result of the investigations, and also with the letters received, and desires to recommend the cause of the negro race, as represented by him, to the sympathy of the public." At the close of the proceedings, Mr. Stanford, addressing those present, said he thought the difficulties and prejudices which he had in the past to battle with were gradually being removed, and that in the future more favour and sympathy would be shown towards the cause which he represented. A working committee was formed, at the suggestion of Mr. Stanford, to receive donations and subscriptions received by him, to be forwarded to the head-quarters in Canada.—*Bradford Telegraph*, Sept. 10th, 1884.

The Committee having been formed, I set to work in earnest, and, on invitation, obtained my transfer, and became a member of the Ripley Street Baptist Chapel, Bradford. I had, however, great difficulty in obtaining employment, and with most of my time unoccupied, I procured a small collection of popular works and endeavoured to sell them, in order to earn something, but for months I did not earn my bread, and for weeks I had nothing but porridge to live upon. I was not without two or three pounds in my pocket, but as I considered it did not belong to me, I scrupulously refrained from spending any of it. I had always a great dread of debt, and I believe I have never contracted one without a fair prospect of discharging it. I have incurred liabilities for printing to some considerable amount since my arrival in England, but my first thought on receiving money was my creditors. On March 1st, 1886, I again visited Barnsley, and there made a number of new acquaintances; and, by their invitation, delivered a lecture on March 3rd.

It was at this time that the writing of "The Story of my Life" was suggested. Besides the hope that such a work would prove useful and instructive to many young people, it was thought that it would answer the purpose of affording information concerning myself, and to obtain which I was constantly subjected to a series of questions by every new set of friends I found. Experience has proved that it has fulfilled the intended purpose admirably, as it answers all reasonable questions concerning myself and my mission to England, and has afforded me and the society for which I was engaged a fair percentage for the trouble and outlay involved in the undertaking.

I afterwards severed my official connection with the Amherstberg Baptist Association and determined to remain in England on my own account. Many thousands of the Story of My Life had been sold under the auspices of the Bradford Committee, but some thousands were still left. These the Committee handed over to me when I left the North, giving me full liberty to deal with the proceeds of the sale of them at my own descretion.

CHAPTER XIII.

I AM "CAST DOWN, BUT NOT DESTROYED."

In June, 1887, I left Bradford and came to Birmingham, where I met one who, by her piety and ardent zeal for Christ, won my heart, and on the 18th August, 1888, we were united in marriage, and her example and affection have made me a better and happier man.

I attended the annual meeting of the Midland Baptist Association, held at Stafford, in June, 1888, and was there introduced to the Rev. Charles Joseph,

Pastor of the Victoria Street Baptist Chapel, Small Heath. I had previously heard of him, but this, I afterwards found out, was not to know him; for after he had taken a careful survey of me, he came forward, and grasping my hand, expressed the pleasure he felt in meeting one of whom he had heard. "Truly," he said, "God has made of one blood all nations of men to dwell upon the face of the earth, and you are my brother." He gave me a cordial invitation to visit him at his house, as he desired to speak to me, promising to gladly render me any service he could; and a few days afterwards I attended a revival meeting and heard him speak. By his invitation I attended three meetings, and spoke at each. At my request, Mr. Joseph procured my letter of transfer from Bradford, and my dear wife and I were received as members at Small Heath. I must here acknowledge my great indebtedness to the Rev. Chas. Joseph, whose kindness and assistance to me have been of the most cordial and helpful character. Having satisfied himself as to my past history and acquirements, he has been unremitting in his attention to me, and indefatigable in his instruction. His home has been the home of myself and wife; and his bearing, and that of the noble christian woman, his wife, towards us, has been one of uniform kindness—not patronage—and Christian brotherhood. The same spirit, I am bound to say, has been shown by the congregation. Truly, as is the pastor, so are the people. I regret to say that such has not been my constant experience during the six years I have been in England. In too many instances the expressions of sympathy I have received have been without any result, and were simply used to serve a selfish purpose, or no purpose. Their sympathy was often shown only in word and not in deed. They used the word simply as it stands in the dictionary, often forgetting the Spirit. I have been shunned, slighted, traduced, and even actively opposed in my efforts to preach the Gospel of Christ; and this treatment I have received at the hands of members of Christian churches, and professed preachers of the gospel. Some of these have thus acted on mere rumour, who have never seen me or spoken to me. Is this the Spirit of Christ? Methinks in that day the "King shall answer and say unto all such: 'Verily I say unto you, inasmuch as you have done it unto one of the least of these my brethren, ye have done it unto me." (Matt. xxv., 40.)

During the past twelve months, I have been anxiously endeavouring to better fit myself for the work of assisting my brethren in Africa. I took the chair at a lecture given in the Lecture Hall of Victoria Street Baptist Chapel, Birmingham, delivered by our highly esteemed brother, the Rev. J. Jenkin Brown, his subject being—"The Congo and its Martyrs"; and this led me to read a book published by the Baptist Missionary Society, called "The Rise and Progress of the Work on the Congo River." Now, from the attention I have given to this subject, I unhesitatingly say that we are sending the wrong men to do the work in Africa, and that if Africa is to be evangelised, it is by a native agency only that the work can be accomplished. We have in the United States of America and Canada 7,747,990 negroes, of whom 2,300,000 are Christians. It is possible to educate them; and that they are better able to stand the climate of Africa than any other race, has been proved by such men as Rev. Bishop Crowther, of the Church Missionary Society, now labouring in West Africa; J. J. Fuller and—. Richardson, of the Baptist Missionary Society, and by members of the Wesleyan Methodist and other Societies. Past experience has convinced me that if we are to educate the coloured men who are now in the States and Canada for African work, we must have an institution specially established for the purpose, and that it should be in touch with English Foreign Missionary Societies. Canada belongs to England; then why not establish an institution there? In furtherance of this object, I wrote a few weeks ago to the Secretary of the African Baptist Association, and his reply has determined me that something shall be done in the matter, and if they will work upon my suggestion we shall have an Institution for such work.

CHAPTER XIV.

I AM PASTOR OF AN ENGLISH BAPTIST CHURCH, WITH MY GOOD NAME VINDICATED BEFORE THE WORLD.

On May 8th, 1889, I received and accepted the following Call from the Baptist Church, Hope Street, Birmingham:

Baptist Church, Hope Street, Birmingham,
May 8th, 1889.

To the Rev. P. T. Stanford.

Revd. and Dear Sir,

At a meeting on Wednesday, May the 8th, it was unanimously decided that we, the members and congregation attending the above place of worship, invite you to become our Pastor. You know our condition will not allow us to offer you a large salary, but we offer you our prayers, willing hearts, and hands. Remember, dear Brother, this call is from God, and He has promised to supply all our needs. Trusting you will see your way to accept our offer.

We are, yours faithfully,

Signed on behalf of the Church,

> D. BRILEY.
>
> H. SMITH.
>
> T. BARBER.
>
> J. MADDOCKS.
>
> H. GREENHILL.
>
> HENRY RICHARDS.
>
> JAS. CLARK, Secretary.

I was not allowed to take my position however until after a stern fight in which, through the grace of God and the kindness of the Rev. Chas. Joseph, and my solicitor, A. T. Carr, Esq., of Birmingham. I at last came off more than conquerer. And to-day, notwithstanding my birth as a slave and the colour of my skin, I am pastor in this great city of Birmingham. I have been libelled, slandered, ostracised, suspected, and opposed; but in all these troubles I have not lacked many true christian friends, whose names my gratitude prompts me to print here, only I know too well that any public mention of their virtues or their deeds of love would but offend their finer susceptibilities. I therefore forbear, and giving thanks to God, bid adieu to my readers with the following, to me, most fitting lines:

> I my Ebenezer raise,
> To my kind Redeemer's praise;
> With a grateful heart I own—
> Hitherto Thy help I've known.
> What may be my future lot,
> Well I know concerns me not,
> This should set my heart at rest:
> What Thy will ordains in best.

Published 1889

J. E. CASELY HAYFORD

Joseph Ephraim Casely Hayford (1866–1930) was born into a prominent Western-educated family in Cape Coast, at that time in the British colony of the Gold Coast, today Ghana. He studied law in Britain and became a journalist and editor in the Gold Coast, the owner of several local newspapers, as well as a co-owner of the London-based *African Times and Orient Review*. He was a vociferous protester against certain aspects of colonial rule, a member of the Gold Coast Aborigines' Rights Protection Society, a founder of the National Congress of British West Africa and one of the leading politicians in the Gold Coast. *Ethiopia Unbound*, one of the first modern African novels, was partly autobiographical and published during one of his many visits to Britain. It was concerned with 'race emancipation', developing African identity and countering Eurocentrism. The following extract is set in London and gives an indication of how some of these themes are explored and presented within the novel.

Ethiopia Unbound: Studies in Race Emancipation

When Whitely parted with Kwamankra, the latter made his way to Holborn and wandered aimlessly down Oxford Street, his mind full of varied thoughts. He had always been a thinker, and this morning in his conversation with Whitely fresh avenues of thought had opened up in his mind which he wished to pursue undisturbed. As he watched the mighty procession of men, women, and children jostling one another, he was overwhelmed with a sense of the weariness which European civilisation had evolved for itself. But it was of the teaching of the Christian philosophy and its paradoxes that his mind was full. Was it not the Nazarene who said: "Come unto me all ye that are weary and heavy laden, and I will give you rest"? Had he given this people, who professed to be his followers, rest in their constant attempt to overreach one another, in the way they trampled upon one another unto fame and fortune? Again, he had called all his followers brethren, and was not his the injunction to go forth and teach all nations that all might be brethren? And, even now, the words of Silas Whitely, Divinity scholar of Queen's: "What a strange question! Our Lord born of an Ethiopian woman!"—again rang in his ears. What if bishops, prelates, in the direct line of Him, Who made Himself of no reputation, felt the same, and yet dared to propagate his gospel among the Ethiopian Gentiles? Were there to be paradoxes all the way through? A religion which taught one thing, and practised another, was it worth following? And in his inmost heart he found himself thanking the gods that he was a poor benighted pagan according to the formula of the Church.

In the frame of mind in which Kwamankra was, he was in no temper to be disturbed; but as luck would have it, he had not gone far when he saw coming towards him a dark man, known among his fellows as the Professor. He professed all things, and knew nothing in particular. He was in reality Kwow Ayensu, a student of several years' standing at the Charing Cross Hospital, to whom, as far as one could judge, the question of a medical or a surgical diploma was of a secondary consideration. Kwamankra dodged the Professor, and made for the opposite pavement. The Professor as promptly crossed over, and familiarly tapping him on the shoulder, said in a gruff voice, "Hallo! old fellow, how are you? I have not seen you for quite an age; and what is the meaning of cutting an old chum like this, eh?"

Evidently there was no getting away from the

Professor, and so Kwamankra resigned himself to his fate.

"The fact is," said Kwamankra, "if you want me to be frank with you, I wanted to be alone. I was so enjoying myself before you interrupted me. I love to observe without being observed."

"Do you include in your observations that of humanity in general?" dryly put in the Professor.

"Yes," replied Kwamankra. "To me it is the most interesting study, and the best theatre I find to be these very pavements, the performers being the moving throng of men and women. To study humanity in this guise is to me the acme of intellectual pastime, and much as I would like a chat with you another time, I am really sorry you disturbed me."

"Your case," said the Professor, "is a simple one of cerebral contraction of the sympathies. Come with me, old boy, to the Argyle Rooms tonight, and I warrant you the finest study of humanity anywhere in London. You may notice without being noticed, and if you should feel inclined to thaw, by Jove! you will have your work cut out. Some of the latest arrivals are rare bits, and they are the rage of all the young hounds, misnamed men. Do come with me."

"I thank you for the kind invitation, but I am afraid I cannot come to the Argyle Rooms with you to-night, as I must catch the night train to Cambridge with a friend."

"Well, then, come with me to the York Hotel instead. It may be I shall be able to interest you, and, if you please, you may stand me a treat after. I hear some of you 'varsity chaps are very good that way. Your average rusty London student does not understand champagne suppers and that kind of thing."

"If it comes to that, Professor, we needn't go all the way to the York Hotel. We can just drop in at Slater's round the corner, and I will warrant you as good a lunch as you ever tasted. Come along now. I will take no refusal."

It did not take much to persuade the Professor, and together they were soon seated at a well-appointed table in a comfortable corner. After lunch the Professor said to Kwamankra, "One good turn deserves another. I thought I would give you a bit of a surprise, but since the mountain would not come to Mahomet, I suppose he must go to it. The fact is, Mansa is in London, and is staying at the York Hotel with her father."

Published 1889

SARAH PARKER REMOND

Sarah Parker Remond (1826–1894) was born in Salem, USA, to a prominent African American family of abolitionists. Her childhood experiences of racism led her to also become an abolitionist lecturer at the age of sixteen, an anti-racist activist and later a campaigner for women's suffrage. She arrived in Britain in 1858 and lectured throughout England, Scotland and Ireland. She studied at Bedford College and University College, London, and was a leading member of the London Emancipation Society. During and after the American Civil War, Remond campaigned in opposition to the Confederacy and in support of the rights of African Americans. In London, she qualified as a nurse and remained in Britain until 1867 when she moved to Italy, married, studied medicine and practiced as a doctor for over twenty years. Her letter to a London newspaper, as shown in the following extract, in the wake of the famous 1865 Morant Bay Rebellion in Jamaica, gives an indication of both her militant style and her anti-racism.

Letter to the Editor of the
London Daily News

5 Trafalgar Square
Brompton, S.W.
[London, England]
[November 7, 1865]

Sir:

Will you allow me to say a word in defence of the most hated race in the world, the negroes and their descendants? Notwithstanding the attempt on the part of our enemies, I think it will be difficult to prove that the negroes are more savage than other races. Unprejudiced observers from time to time have given facts which prove that the negroes, under similar circumstances, are as humane as the dominant races. Now, take for granted, if you please—I do not—that all the cruelties reported during the recent insurrection in Jamaica are true: take also for granted that the negroes are entirely the aggressors, and I appeal to every candid mind to answer this question, whether the aggressors would have been dealt with in so summary a manner if they had belonged to the dominant race, and their complexions had been white instead of black? It has been with feelings of intense gratitude that the colored race have turned with confidence to one fact, i.e.,

84

that since the decision of Lord Mansfield, in 1772, every human being, without any reference whatever to a difference of complexion, was an equal before the law. If they committed any crime, they expected to be legally tried and punished. But there is a change in the public opinion in Great Britain in reference to the colored race. There are many causes for this change, and for which the colored race are in no way to blame. Attacks as ungenerous as they are unjust are made upon the negro race and their descendants. The "West Indian interest" always had this hatred towards a race they had oppressed. This conduct shocked the moral sense of the better portion of the English people, and slavery was forced to yield. Since the civil war in the United States, the Southern Confederates and their natural allies, these former West Indian planters, have united together to endeavor to neutralize the interest felt for the oppressed negroes, and to hold them up to the scorn and contempt of the civilized world. No matter what a colored man may do—whether it is a crime committed, or some slight impropriety, it is exaggerated, and noticed in the most insulting manner. I have read the pro-slavery newspapers in the United States with most careful attention for more than a quarter of a century, but I have never read more insulting attacks upon the negro race than I have read within the last four years in some of the London journals. Within the last month, I have read attacks upon the negro race which would disgrace any Southern Confederate or negrohating Northerner. We are expected to be not only equal to the dominant races, but to excel in all that goes toward forming a noble manhood or womanhood. We are expected to develop in the highest perfection a race which for eight generations in the United States has been laden with the curse of slavery. Even some of our friends seem to expect this, but our enemies demand it. Now, take the four and a half millions of "freedmen" in the States, and consider the present attempts made by our enemies to prove that they are unfitted for freedom. I ask the English public to investigate the facts in reference to negro character, as developed there during the present century, and particularly during the civil war. Compare their character in reference to cruelty with their masters, "the chivalry of the South," who for eight generations have mutilated their slaves, and not unfrequently during the present generation burnt their victims to death; who, in the words of one of your own countrymen, "notch the ears of men and women, cut pleasant poesies in their shrinking flesh, learn to write with pens of red-hot iron on the human face, rack their poetic fancies for liveries of mutilation which their slaves shall wear for life, and carry with them to the grave." Our cup of bitterness is more than full. If negroes or colored men commit crime in Jamaica, or anywhere else, exact the full penalty, but do not make it the occasion of the most insulting and unjust attacks upon a whole race, on account of a difference of complexion.

I am, &c.,

SARAH P. REMOND

Daily News (London), 22 November 1868.

THEODORE THOMAS

The author of *Hard Truth* is almost certainly S. J. Celestine Edwards (*c.*1857–1894), originally from Dominica. He became the first person of Caribbean heritage to become a newspaper editor and publisher in Britain. From 1880, Edwards first settled in Edinburgh and Sunderland and worked in a variety of occupations before becoming a lay preacher and a speaker on temperance and anti-secularism. Moving to London, he studied theology and medicine, and travelled throughout the country as a popular lecturer. His speeches increasingly assumed an anti-racist and anti-imperialist orientation. He became a leading figure in the Quaker-led Society for the Recognition of the Brotherhood of Man, editor of its publication *Fraternity* and, in 1893, an organizer of the anti-lynching lecture tour of Britain by African American Ida B. Wells. *Hard Truth* is presented as a debate between Christ and Lucifer. This extract presents the argument that Britain is the birthplace of anti-African racism.

Hard Truth

My object in presenting this little book to the public is to tell the naked Truth, and this may be considered by many a most bold thing for me to do. There are moments, though, in the lives of most men when all the power of their better nature forces them to speak the Hard Truth. And after many years of going in and out among the nations of Europe, that time of life has come to me.

I would, though, that it had not come—forced upon me in the way and place that it has. Some say that it is not always best to tell the Truth, because it has "killed" so many. Everyone knows that Christ never would have been crucified had he not told the Truth. It is not my intention to bless any denomination of Christians; neither is it my intention to ask sympathy for my people; then what they want is, Justice! And every right-thinking man or Christ-like Church in this or any country knows that no gold or farm seekers will ever give justice to a people of whom dislike has been (even from Christian ministers) imbibed into their very souls since so many generations. It is second nature to the sons of Britain to dislike, to be prejudiced to, and (often) hate the Negro. And has he ever done them any harm? What

I do ask of Church, Christian, and Man is, to demand of his or her Government to mete out *humane justice* to the people it conquers, and not to allow all their goods and chattels to be taken from them, and then force them to "come in" and till the raped soil for the conquerors. Is not that reducing them to slavery? If the reader wishes to see humane justice queen upon the earth, I would that he remember that whoso helps on such a reign is much nearer Heaven than the character in this book which tells the Hard Truth.

The first chapter of the book serves as an introduction to "Hard Truth," the greater part of which the writer has witnessed.

THEODORE THOMAS

[. . .]

BRITONS LEAD THE WORLD.

LUCIFER: It is not my wish to tempt you; why should I? Is not all this mine? And if I offer you a part of it does that not show how much I like you? I am not one of those who forget "Auld Lang Syne." Why an English pork butcher, who, having made his fortune by selling chopped-up pigs, might find it difficult to pass one of these Jew-hated quadrupeds without raising his hat to him. If, then, a pork butcher so reverently remember the worth and spirit of pigs, is it possible for a great spirit like mine to forget the Divine Spirit, before which it has always had much respect? Why, Emanuel, I would divide with you to the half of my kingdom, on condition that I have control of both halves! If you wish to remain on earth you must serve me. *I will be first.* Selfishness is my nature; and when I am good with one hand, it is with the weaker hand, and only with the little finger of that hand; and I have, and shall ever, imbibe self and selfishness into the very soul of the most cultured nations of the universe; and these are those who know best your doctrine: Britons leading!

II.

I am sorry we had not time to stop a few hours in Britain, because I should have been most pleased had you seen the birth place of Livingstone. And I would have been glad, for a little reason of my own, had you studied the ground where comes the nasty, tough shrub which grows to a great tree in America, India, Australia, here in Africa, and everywhere where your Word is (especially in the English language) preached. You have said that I am a "liar," but I will tell you another truth, which you know well, but that some would rather not have it said.

When Light tells a truth it is an electric one. Here's my truth: Britain is the birth-place of the very essence of the seed of prejudice against the negro race. And the little uncouth, rough shrub, when transplanted from its mother country, grows into a great tree in Gentile lands. And I have ordered all the hosts of Hell—the noble princes who fought with me against you and your Father—to water that tree until its summit touches and defies Heaven, and until its roots reach the bottom of the foundation of Hades. *It is done.* And if Paul should rise up from the dead, and begin his powerful preaching for you, he could not uproot that tree. There are a few Britons, though, good, as if fresh out of the mould of God. But, hark! listen to that fine music in the air! See, yonder on the Walls of Heaven, that Shining Host. There is Paul, the faithful soldier; and Helen, the woman among ten thousand; and old Cæsar, still wearing on his breast the words, "The stone which the builders rejected." And see there, near the Gate, old bald-head Peter, with the Key in his hand. Oh! that I could swell the ocean to the very sill of yon impregnable fortress, raise up the engulfed tars and their beloved ironclads, and batter down the Gate with my big guns and walk into Heaven *victori*—

CHRIST: Enough, Destruction!

LUCIFER: I beg pardon, Emanuel; I was

getting a bit excited. Don't pay any attention to what I said about capturing Heaven. You know that I cannot turn the earth's course, because your Father has ordered it; neither can I swell up the ocean beyond its bounds, because your Father has hemmed it. I am supreme only *over all flesh*. But thou art looking tired. Come, let us go up to the top of that mount there, where that time-worn long rock is, and we shall have a splendid view of all the valley and country round about. Now, this is better! Sit down there on the end of the stone, and I will take my place, stradle of it, behind you. What a beautiful and peaceful country this is. It is really too beautiful for one to wear such a long, sorrowful face as you do. Cheer up! Look! See there! Those are my brave Britons arranging their laager; and here to the right are the Matabeles, living either their last day of freedom or their last day on earth. They are nearly a mile off, and they have begun to shoot. Why, a good English marksman would count himself lucky if he touched, from that distance, the House of Parliament with one of those guns. The Chartered Company, after having persuaded Lobengula to sign something that he could not read, and which has since disappeared, gave him the half-got-up guns as a remuneration. And they will take them all back after the battle. I mean to say that the conditions of peace will be, that all Matabeles give up their arms, their land, and cattle, and come—if they wish to remain in the land—and till it for these sons of Britain. And I assure you that the negro will scarcely be paid enough to keep, even in this country, soul and body together. See how the naked men rush on to death. The Chartered Company has opened fire on them with my big guns. See how the blacks fall into the arms of death. Still they rush on! What brave men to fight against such odds! Why, not one-third of them have even one of those bad small guns the Company made for them, and there is not a cannon on their side. Still they rush on, and see how they fall. The Britons are laughing at their bravery. If this were at the Battle of Waterloo, they would say, "Surrender yourselves." But this is a battle of extermination. These are the sons of Anglo-Saxon-and-Norman blood—"blue blood"—of Southern rights and hopes drying up the reservoir of negro blood. See that officer there, how deliberately he takes aim and fires? He thinks he is out deer-shooting. The Matabeles see that they cannot stand against such odds, and the few that are left are fleeing. The officer is going to get on his horse. There now, he has stepped on that little stone and sprained his ankle. Someone will say that he deserves the "Victoria Cross" for that. All the cavalry and foot troops are out shooting them down without any mercy. Do you see them? And there winds the rivulet of negro blood down the valley. The reservoir has been well re-tapped this time. Don't weep, Emanuel; I know you would have gathered that blood together, in the flesh, as a hen gathers her brood, but your Church would not. There are a few, though, who say that Lobengula is a good man, and that he treats the whites well. There was even a white who wished to go to the king and explain to him the odds of the "war" with the Britons, but the chief of these white men would not allow him to do it. He wishes the black men's "coat" and "cloak," too, and he is going to have both. Look at that herd of cattle the Britons are driving in to be divided among these sons of the Island of Christian Churches—land of Clarkson, Wilberforce, Lord Shaftesbury, and your servant, Livingstone. Yes, yon little island has stopped kidnapping the negro to sell him into slavery, to kidnap his land and his cattle, which are all the wealth he has. You have seen that yourself to-day. Your Church and people have set their seal against this people, and all the power in Heaven cannot keep the two in one from making slaves of them in some way or from killing them. Missionary work among them is nothing but a great shame as far as you are concerned. It suits me, though. Here is the way it is done. The missionaries tell their Government *all* about the country where they have their missions; then the Government tells the people and the Church, and these three—inseparable trinity— which are ten million times more zealous in advancing the Kingdom of England than they are in advancing the Kingdom of God, come with great guns and shoot down the natives (who try to defend themselves with sticks), and then divide the land among themselves, and go home to the Mother Country to be decorated for bravery and good deeds.

III.

Every nation of Europe was represented in the slave markets until a few of your sort of men got round the Christian Church in such a way, and so power- fully, that the people thought the negro ought to be made free. And it was done. A few years later, the great nation in whose language the slave markets were carried on, divided the Negro's Continent (as if it had been one of their own English plum pud- dings) among the Powers of Europe, and then invited them to join her in a blocus on the high seas to stop the slave ships which still found a market for the negro. Then the Great Power said to the Chil- dren Powers: "Germany, that's your part; Italy, you may have yon part; France, we will allow you to have that part there; and we Britons will take this part. But, don't any of you turn to the right or to the left, but go straight forward, there is ample space for you to try the effects of your great guns on human flesh. Kill the 'niggers' as much as you like—we have stopped the slave trade! But if you turn to the right or to the left we shall have a row among ourselves." And here is England killing them by the thousands, Italy rivalling with England, and Germany trying to beat both of these two put together. And France, country of small families, does not need to exterminate them to make room for her own children, kills them by hundreds only.

CHRIST: What does France do?

LUCIFER: France, because she has small families, can afford "to live and let live." But England and Germany, which carry out (to the greater extent of the letter of feminine endurance in travail) your commandment, "Be fruitful and multiply," are obliged to make room somewhere for their superfluous Protestant seed, which protests against the existence of everything else except itself.

IV.

Rome, where she conquered, took hostages to her capital, and treated them kindly—she did not lock up the young princes of the conquered land in St. Helena's dungeons, neither hated she those that she conquered, but mingled with them and taught them civilisation. What do your people do? They come, conquer, take, divide, and reduce to serfdom (slavery) the few natives upon whom the great guns had pity; and a British Christian gentleman will go all over England telling the people that it was, and is, a "national necessity," because Britain needed a place for her—unemployed! The Zulu "war," was it anything like a just one? Britons themselves say it was not. Yet they sent a fryer into the land to fry all the Zulus up; and when he had finished his great, noble, and immortal work his country sent all the princes of the conquered land to prison. And the truly noble British woman, who plead their cause, and who told her compatriots how unjust it is to shut them up in St. Helena's dungeons and treat them badly, has disappeared, or we hear her no more speak. But her Mother Country is sending someone here to-day to make roads over the Matabeles. The King Lobengula knows from the fate of the Zulu king, Cetewayo, and the princes of his family, what British justice means to an African chief, so he left a few days ago, knowing that he could not fight against such terrible odds. Here in Africa the accuser, who is always an Englishman, answers before the British Government for himself and for the accused. And you know that in such cases the unheard man is always a liar and a villain. "It is easy to vanquish the non-combatants." Professions and arts should have no nationality. Some of the natives here may, after a few years, go to Britain to study medicine, and when they shall have finished their course of study, the noble professor, who sees nothing in man but blood and brains, may congratulate them as he hands them their diploma or *doctorat*. Some of their white colleagues will applaud them for having had sense enough to pass in the English language such difficult examinations; others will applaud the speech of the professor, and the rest will applaud the exit of the negroes from among them. A few men and women of the working classes, to whom they may have given medical aid in hospitals, will meet them at the door of the university or medical college, and, from hearts as free from prejudice as Heaven, say, "Doctor, don't leave us; we like you." And their little children will run after them, and take them by the hand and whisper, "Good-bye, doctor." And the "Upper Ten," looking out of their windows, will say, "Hurry up, old blackies, or niggers (according to school or parents), and get back where you came from; we wouldn't have you in our houses if we were dying, and keep out of the way of the Maxim guns if you can." The negroes return home, or to some other country, and find the little shrub around which they walked in Britain grown to be a great tree. Let them go where they may in this world they will find that tree, and if they make even their bed in——I will burn that tree up! There is no respect of persons with me.

V.

Twenty years ago Britain was quite different towards the negro to what she is to-day. The Old Country though had freed the slaves in Jamaica several years previously. I will explain. Some good men, all of whom are dead now, so stirred the Britons up for freedom during the war in the States, that they had not, twenty years ago, given over rejoicing about Lincoln's Proclamation of Emancipation. And even Manchester—big, dirty, smoky, wealthy Manchester—which had suffered so very much during the Yankee war (because of the scarcity of cotton for her great mills), did not possess a hall large enough to contain the thousands who had come to hear and to welcome ten black singers. And if a negro singer go to the same city to-day, the music dealer refuses to sell him music at professional prices. And sing he at a great seaside resort in Lanca-shire, many of the musicians of the band will sneer at him, and play all sorts of drunken accords when he sings—"And God created man." There was living, though, twenty years ago, not far from Manchester, a Christian (who belonged to that Church which *has* been a thorn in the side of all the other Churches), and he threw bright light all over the country round about him. But he is dead now, and with John Bright vanished much humane light. It is thus that I quickly bring all things that you love to be subservient to my will. I have even heard it said that there are men in England who would not care a pin if Wilberforce's monument in Hull was razed to the ground. In fact, I have succeeded so well in my position behind you, that I could lie down and sleep a hundred years, and wake up at the end of that time and find my work going on so well by your Church that the noble princes of Hades would cry out: "They are working too fast, oh, thou greatest of Emperors!" But I am not going to sleep! After you are gone, I am going back to England to see the Britons black their faces to buffoon the negro in their theatres, halls, streets, and at all the watering-places. How high will you raise a man up if you only try to lift him up with the little finger of your left hand, and then, with all the strength of your right hand and arm, you knock him down? Would you think that this buffooning of the negro was done to ease the task of the Board School (and other) teachers? The negro, Emanuel, must be hated, and there is no use you standing there thinking that your Church is going to love him. Why, if one find a friend, even in Britain, where is only found the tough, rough shrub of prejudice, people wonder if the white man has gone crazy by admitting into his house a black man. And if the Briton die, members of his family (come from afar) will insult the negro as he administers to his white friend's dying wants and needs, and when the negro leaves the house of mourning a little white man, with great newspapers under his arms, and a *coiffeur royale*, laugh at him, and add injury to insult throughout the whole town. The Society for the Recognition of the Brotherhood of Man might as well stop pleading to your Church—that is to say, to your modern Chosen People—to be just towards the negro, and the editor of *Fraternity*, might as well cease beseeching his race and people to take their foot off the negro's neck, and give *him a chance to get up.* "Might is Right!"

VI.

Look at that big lion coming down the hill yonder, towards the rivulet of African blood; see how stately he walks, the king of beasts! Why, he is drinking from the rivulet of blood; how fast he swallows it down. He has raised his head to take breath, and is walking backwards. Why, he has jumped over this side. It seems that he thought the blood better on our side, and has sprung over to taste it. See how his sides are swollen out with it, yet he keeps lapping it up, the glutton! Now he has laid himself down to sleep; but what a restless sleep he seems to be in? What can be the matter with him? Listen! he roared in his sleep, and has awaked and turned himself over in springing position. See how he grabs the earth in his great paws, and looks as if he would like to fasten the whole world in them. What is he looking at? Ah! I see now; it is the great bear coming down that hill there to your right. The great monster is waggling straight to the lion, and does not seem at all afraid. He has stopped to suck his foot, and seems to hesitate. Now he has got up, and waddles slowly on, and looks as if he were trying to elude the lion. But see how he promenades up and down before the king of beasts, getting closer and closer to him at every turn. Now he has stopped and raised himself up on his hind feet, and the lion is going to spring on him; there he flies through the air, and the bear has caught him on his left fore-leg, and with his right paw has opened his bowels! See how the blood is flowing; negro blood! Now the bear has stopped squeezing him, and has thrown him on the ground, and has smelt him, and pronounced a doctor's sentence on him—Dead. That was a fairer fight than the one between the English and Matabeles, although the bear would not have had a chance had he caught the lion while he was in the air. I like a fair fight—so do Britons at home—but the fight between the English and Africans can well be likened to a "war" between an English kindergarten school of children from three to six years old and one of these strong Africans. There would be just as much chivalry in such a "war" as there is in this one which you have seen before you to-day. What are you thinking about now? There is no use you hoping that a G.O.M. is going to bring in a Bill of "Home Rule" for the Africans! Why such a Bill would not remain even a half-day in the House of Commons, and the Lords of Britain never would allow it to pass the threshold of their door.

VII.

I see you believe in the number, Three! The Roman Catholic Church came out of the catacombs and became a great power for selfishness, reached its *apogee*, and fell humbled to the earth. So humble is it that it is the only "white man's Church" where, in some parts of the "Christian world," negroes are admitted. Out of the ruins of this humbled Church was born the Protestant Church, which grew up quickly, waxed strong, whipped her mother, and took all from her she could, and founded herself on slavery and destruction. Look at her, to-day, the insatiable, gluttinous girl, armed to her very teeth, holding in her hand the sword that spills blood and gives death, and trampling in the dust the Sword of Jesus of Nazareth—your sword—which gives life. "I will have farms, big farms, for my brothers," says this ravenous daughter of the Roman Catholic Church. And you have seen here, her brothers, before your eyes, shooting the—as they will write to their tender-hearted mothers and sisters—"niggers down like dogs," while thousands on bended knee are praying to thee for success of big farms and gold mines. Gold, Emanuel, is the god here of your Church and Chosen People. Why, even Gœthe, the great German writer, said, "Die Kirche hat ganze Länder abgefressen und hat nie genug" the Church has swallowed up whole lands and has never enough. When Matabeleland shall have been divided according to the will of the Chartered Company, and false papers shall have been sent to the Government in London, some good brother in your Church will come and preach "Benevolence" to the Matabeles, and their education in Sunday and day schools will be, "Servants. obey your masters!" Two hundred years ago, Britons were here shooting down and kidnapping the negroes to sell them for gold. One hundred years ago, Clarkson and Wilberforce plead so well the negro's cause that during a few hours you might have thought all Britain to be like *you*. The slaves were freed in Britain's Colonies, and left to the mercy of (and solely depending upon) the Britons who had degraded them. Were the twenty millions given to the slaves? Thirty years ago the descendants of Britain in North America gave back to the negroes their God-given right, and thought they had done thereby their (Heaven-worthy) duty to them, and that it was just not to allow them anything for their unrequited toil, and to leave them to the mercy of their ex-masters, the greatest and worst enslavers that ever breathed. And here we see to-day the British Government—not content with its great Empire upon which the sun never sets— authorising a greedy company of men to destroy these negroes, and laughing to scorn anyone, be he even an M.P., who dares speak in their behalf. The Britons first sent missionaries to talk to them of thy love; and, to-day, instead of sending *canons* of your Church here to preach to them *God's Word*, they are sending *cannons* here to preach *my word*, and they have done it too well. Never, Emanuel, has anything served me so well as your Church. You may have thought that, after having wronged these people during so many years, your Church, and more especially the British part of it, would have given the negroes more than *a superhuman chance*. Vain thought, Emanuel; give the whole thing up, and be happy. Then prejudice, hatred, greed, and buffoonery never elevated any people, neither have they ever given *prestige* in "Board Schools."

Published 1894

JOHN OCANSEY

John Emanuel Ocansey (?–1889) was the adopted
son of William Ocansey, a wealthy import and
export merchant in what was then the Gold Coast
(Ghana), and the husband of the latter's daughter.
It was reported that John was originally of Fulani
origin and initially a slave in the Ocansey household,
but there is little certainty about his early life or date
of birth. He represented his adopted father at an
important legal case in Britain and thereby came to
write not only an account of the case and of his
father's trading difficulties, but more importantly
the reflections of an African visiting Britain for
the first time. His brief memoirs include his recollections of London, Liverpool, Manchester and
Southport. The extracts included here present Ocansey's impressions of Britain's railways, London's main
tourist attractions and Manchester's Zoological Gardens, as well as attitudes towards begging and the
casual racism that he experienced in the street.

An African Trading, Or the Trials of William Narh Ocansey, of Addah, West Coast of Africa, River Volta

On the 19th we reached Madeira in the evening. This is another great mountain in the ocean; but it is larger and more beautiful and more fruitful than the other two. I went ashore that night, though it was after seven o'clock, but it was as light as noonday, and continued so as I passed leisurely through the fine streets with their light houses, so that I did not recognise the night to be night, but just as the day.

When we were about three days' sail from Liverpool we began to see lighthouse vessels and iron buoys with tells and lights upon them, and they are so anchored out in the sea that they form a kind of road for the vessels to pass in. We had now been out from Madeira eight days, and it was a great delight for us to reach the river Mersey, at Liverpool, on the 27th day of May. And oh! what a busy, wonderful sight it was! Along the river sides are the docks and these were all full of steamers and sailing ships; and their masts stood out like a forest of trees with no leaves on them. And the river, too, was full of vessels at anchor, and moving constantly up and down and backwards and forwards. I saw a very large one with four masts and four chimneys, and another one, almost square, with paddles, filled with hundreds of live cattle, bringing them out the wide and deep river. Indeed they appeared to me in all sizes and in all shapes, and were too wonderful for me to describe here. For I was told there were about six thousand in and about the river.

When we had cast our anchor in the river, a steam launch with two chimneys, called a tender came alongside (for our vessel was not going into dock then), and received all our thirty-two passengers and their luggage, and took us to the landing stage, where we landed, and all our boxes were taken into a large Government room to be examined by the custom-house officers. It was said there were 200 of them, all dressed in uniform. The boxes are opened for them, and they put their hands down into them to feel if there is anything that should pay the customs duties, and where they find there is not, they close the box and put a chalk mark upon it and you can then take it away and go to your lodgings.

And now, when the voyage was over and all the dangers past, I felt a deep sense of gratitude to my Heavenly Father for his kind protection. I had often heard of the dangers of the mighty deep sea – of the strong and violent winds that raised the waves mountains high – of the vessels plunging and labouring against the raging elements, and the sailors being at their wits end; and I had an especial dread of the terrible Bay of Biscay: But we had come along our great journey as if we had been on a summer trip; and I had escaped from sea sickness and from all fear of danger.

"I'll praise my Maker while I've breath,
And when my eyes are lost in death,
    Praise shall employ my nobler powers:
My days of praise shall ne'er be past,
While life, or thought, or being last,
    Or immortality endures."

When I first walked through the streets of Liverpool I thought it was a feast day, because every man and woman I met appeared so well and nicely dressed. So I asked what feast it was to-day that caused everybody to be dressed up and walking about. But I was quickly told it was not a feast, but the usual style and custom of the place, and that if anyone would dare to go without being dressed, they would be punished by the Government. The next day when I went out I saw it was just the same, and large numbers of ladies, very grandly dressed, were walking about, and stopping to look in the large glass windows of the various shops.

The streets are very broad, and are divided or

shared into three parts. The middle is made with small paving stones, with sand and tar run in between them, to make them smooth and firm; and this is the part for the horses, carts, and carriages. Each side of this is a wide walk covered with smooth flags for the people only to walk on. Many big coaches called "omnibuses," with three and four horses drawing them, run constantly to all parts of the town and to the villages, and the people get inside and on the top. Besides, there are dark streets used only by the railways, that go under the other streets, and they too are crowded with passengers.

Liverpool is a very large city. The length of it, I consider, will be as far as from Addah to Weycoomber and the breadth from Addah to Lolonar all thickly covered with houses. It would be two days of African travel to go from one end to other.

On the first Sunday I was there I went to worship at the Presbyterian Church, Mount Pleasant, which is near to where I lodge. When I went in, I saw a large body of hearers, all the seats seemed full, and the chapel will hold 2,000 people. The church was quite different to any I had ever seen in Africa, and for the first time in my life I saw and heard an organ; I had only known it by its name before. The minister came in and went up the stairs into the pulpit, and gave out the number of the hymn that had to be sung. Then the organ gently and sweetly played over the tune that had to be sung to the hymn. It seemed to me like low and silvery voices. Then the organist pulled out the stops, and played with force and power, and all the people sang together with it, that the sound filled all the church, and it was like as if the angels were singing above. Oh! all my body trembled, and I wanted no one tell me that God was there. The devout and attentive manners which all the people behaved, both great and small, was clear evidence to me that it was God's house.

On the second Sunday, I attended the Methodist Free Church, Russell Street. It was the Sabbath School Anniversary, and all Scholars were arranged on a platform, and sang hymns that they been trained to sing, accompanied by the organ, and oh! how sweet and beautiful they did seem to me! Moreover, I felt more and more and at home here, for I know some of the tunes and the hymns; their way of conducting the service is similar to that of Wesleyans on the Coast. I made many friends in this place of worship. They came to me after the service, and gave me a friendly invitation to dine with the minister at the house of Mr. Looney, Mount Vernon Green, and I spent a most pleasant enjoyable day with the family. Mr. George Quilliam, manufacturer, of Elizabeth Street, was exceedingly kind and obliging, and I am proud to rank him amongst my friends.

When I first came to my lodgings at 24, Oxford Street Liverpool, I was very awkward and shy, but I tried to conceal ignorance and ask no questions. When I first went into my bedroom I did not know how to put the gas out, so I blew at it, and put it out! and got into bed, and fell fast asleep! Now I had done a dangerous thing, and it was by God's providence that I have been preserved. Early the next morning, my landlady, Mrs. Lyle, rose in great haste and alarm, and began to speak loud, and say that the house was full of gas! and she came trembling to my room door said, "Mr. Ocansey, did you blow out the gas last night?" I said "Yes, I did." She exclaimed, "Good God! and she continued, thank God that after that you did not strike or scratch a match; if you had, the house would have been blown to pieces, and all killed. Do you not know that gas is as dangerous as gunpowder. I was amazed, and had to confess that I did not know how to put it out. She then called me to look near to the pipe, and showed me a small screw fastened into it, and she said, "When you want to put out the gas again, don't blow at it, but turn the screw this way and it will go out without danger." I then thanked her, and asked her if there were any other dangerous things in the room? but she said there was nothing more.

On Sunday, the 26th of June, I visited the Blue-coat school where many young orphan boys and girls are taken in and educated. After passing through and inspecting the apartments in which they live, I went into their church to attend the service. It was a large building, capable of holding 2,000 persons, besides all the Blue-coat Scholars, which number about 300, and 100 lady teachers, singers, and servants. The church was very full, and I was told that people come to hear the singing, which is very fine, for the scholars are well trained. After the people were all seated, the organist came in, and began to play a soft, sweet exercise, which I thought to be part of the service. The pulpit was there, but there was no one in it, and I began to feel uneasy about the minister – why did he delay? had he not arrived? was he taken ill? Still the organist went on playing what appeared a long time. But see! Now he pulls out the stops of the organ, and rises to his exercise with great energy, and changes the sound of the organ until it is like a large band of music marching. I could hardly think it was the organ, for I thought I heard many instruments, and the drum beating, and it swelled louder and louder in great deep tones until the place shook with the sound. Then he played a fine march, and the scholars, boys and girls, came marching in, two by two, so close that they touched each other in walking, and kept stop to the music most correctly. Oh how nice and pleasant it was, and how clean and healthy they all appeared! Nothing pleased me more than the large white broad collars over their necks. They came marching on through the middle of the Church with steady, solid step to the tones of the drum-playing organ. Then one little boy, about ten years of age ascended into the pulpit, and taking the hymn-book, gave out the hymn like an aged minister. Then the organist, after preparing his steps, began to play, and all the people rise and sing –

> "Before Jehovah's awful throne,
>   Ye nations, bow with sacred joy;
> Know that the Lord is God alone,
>   He can create and He destroy."

After that, twelve boys came forward in a line just before the organ and pulpit, and one of them, taking a book called a Catechism, asked the others a great many questions, which they answered very willingly, and with great ability. Then six girls came forward, and they were asked many questions out of the Bible, and they also answered very correctly and cleverly. A collection was then made, and afterwards a hymn sung, and the little boy gave the benediction. Then, without the least noise or confusion, they form into procession, and march out to the sound of the organ. We followed them, and passed through their eating rooms. Their evening meal was then prepared and on the tables: their bread on wooden plates, and their tea and milk in tin cups. I was told that they were all poor and destitute children that were taken in, who had no father or mother, and that the expense of keeping them is defrayed by some of the people of the city, who give yearly subscriptions they think fit.

On Sunday, the 1st of July, I attended the Methodist Church, Russell Street, and then I noticed that there were ministers in the pulpit. One, a gentleman, gave out the hymn prayed, and read two lessons from the Bible. Then he retired, a lady came forward, Miss Pooke, about thirty years of age, dressed plainly in black, and looking very modest, but very earnest gave out her text from the Bible, and began to preach in a fluent and excellent style, equal to the best of ministers. On "Abraham offering up Isaac, or personal sacrifices for God."

Liverpool, I have said, is a large place with crowds of people. Down by the docks, and near to where we landed are merchants' offices, very fine, large buildings, built of stone and marble, and five and six stories high. The streets are wide thronged with crowds of people, looking wide awake and earnest, walking fast, and hurrying about as if, they had a great deal of business, and all the shops were well stocked with all kinds of fine things. At night the streets are all lighted up with numerous gas and electric lights, and are as bright as though it were day.

On the day following my arrival, I make enquiries about Hickson, Sykes & Co., and then I found they had been declared bankrupt, and that the 17th of June had been appointed for a meeting of their creditors. This was terrible news. I felt heart sink, and I could not eat for three days. I thought of my dear father and the heavy loss he would sustain of 2,670, because of all the delay in the enlargement of his business for want of steam launch, for which he had already paid, and which ought to have been out and in full working order. I new found that I could do nothing but wait and attend the meeting of creditors. I remembered that I had business in London, and on the 7th of July I decided to visit that great city to see some of my firm's agents. At eleven o'clock in the morning we left Lime Street Station in Liverpool, and arrived in Euston Square Station, London, at 5.30 in the afternoon, travelling at some times at the rate of sixty miles in one hour!

When I first went into the railway train, I observed they were like great coaches, mounted on springs, with strong, heavy wheels. Six persons can sit side by side in a row, and they are so high that a man can stand upright with his hat on and not touch the top. The seats are cushioned, and the carriages have large, strong glass windows at each end, and a lamp at the top to give light when they are rushing through the dark tunnels. Some carriages will carry fifty or more persons, and the carriages can be hooked on, one after the other, according to the number of passengers. A large and powerful engine, with fires burning inside, was fastened to the front of the carriages. The steam was coming out of the top, or chimney, with great force and noise. After I had been inside, and secured my seat, I came out and stood on the platform, near to the door, to look at the large station, and all the people coming and going, and I was greatly astonished to see so large a place. You can walk about for half-an-hour before you can go all round it; and yet this vast place is all covered over with a glass roof. Supported and held up by iron beams and pillars. Whilst I was gazing out a gentleman came up, dressed in a blue suit, with silver buttons. I thought he was a soldier; but he shouted out, "Take your seats gentlemen; show your tickets." I immediately jumped inside, and he took my ticket and made a small cut in it and then shut the door with a loud bang. I then heard a bell ringing, and the engine gave a loud screech, or whistle, and began to move very slowly at first, but gradually increased in speed, and we shot into a dark tunnel, which is made under the houses for about two miles, until we came out into the light in the country. I was bewildered with the motion of the carriages, and the great noise they made in rushing through the tunnel. The carriages were certainly very comfortable, and the lamp in the top gave us good light. But it was pleasant to break out into the sunshine again. Then I settled and composed myself to look out of the window on the country, and behold! all the trees of the field seemed to be flying away from us backwards! It was then I saw how swiftly we were going; swifter than a bird can fly through the sky! And thus the engine rushed and pushed away with all its might; and we went dashing along past houses, villages, and through the midst of large towns, and over high bridges, and darted in and out of deep tunnels, with such a loud noise that I could not hear the sound of my own voice. As I looked out on the country it seemed very green and beautiful. There were many cattle in the fields and all the land is divided by hedges, and long lines of bushes and trees. There were many houses and towns all the way, and large factories with long chimneys.

After we had been flying along in this way for more than four hours, the train began to get quiet and to go slower, until it stopped; and a man, dressed as an officer, came and violently opened the door, and shouted out, "Tickets, please:" and he took them from us; then I knew I was in the great city of London: But I was not tired of the journey, it was so pleasant, and so short a time in coming such a long distance.

I consider the distance from Liverpool to London to be equal in length as from Addah to Cape Coast Castle, and that journey by land takes us fourteen days, and now I have travelled it in four hours and half!

Oh, I do pray that I may live to see one of these railways on the West Coast of Africa: What a saving of time and trouble it will be to the poor Africans, who have to make their long and weary journeys on a foot, carrying their heavy loads on their heads, under a broiling, burning sun! Oh! my God look down in mercy and remember for good the poor Africans, that they also may enjoy the benefits, advantages, and pleasures of knowledge and civilization; Oh! that they would consider and be wise, and rise up like the prodigal son, and say, "I will arise and go to my Father, and will say with him, Father, I have sinned against heaven and before thee, and am no more worthy to be called thy son; make me as one of thy hired servants." And God, our merciful Father, will in no wise cast us out; but He will, instead of servants, make us as His dear children. I have had conversations with many intelligent, high-minded Christian people in England, and they all say that the improvement of the white man is derived from nothing but the word of God. Africa, I hope, will not cast away this most sacred, precious Word, which is now being preached amongst them in very many places by white men. In some places it has been preached for fifty years, in others forty, thirty, twenty, and ten years, and in all it has produced some precious fruit. Oh! may the knowledge of the Lord spread over Africa as the waters cover the great deep! Then shall Africa find out her great health and riches; – then will the earth yield her increase, and God, even our God, shall bless us.

"Come home come home, you are weary at heart;
For the way has been dark, and so lonely and wild;
Oh! prodigal child, come home, oh! come home!

Come home, come home, oh! come home.

"Come home, come home, from the sorrow and blame,
From the sin and the shame, and the tempter that smiled;
Oh! prodigal child, come home, oh! come home!"

Africa is rising – she is lifting up her head, and the Light is spreading. Not many years back, and but few Africans came to Europe, and those who did were generally from Sierra Leone and connected with the government. But now native African traders and their sons from far away up the coast come on their own business, and the kindness shown to them is so great that they are filled with pleasure and gratitude. They are taken to see anything that is useful and profitable, and they are improved and not spoiled. When they return to their friends and neighbours, they have very much to say, and are listened to with respect and confidence. Then their people are proud and pleased that the English have respected them and they are far more ready to accept English ways and customs. And thus, little by little, Africa will be changed, as England was changed; for she too has come out of the darkness into God's marvellous light.

When I got out from the railway train at Euston Square, in London, there was great confusion and noise, and I was for a little time bewildered where to go or what to do. But I went out into the street with the other people, and to an hotel quite near. I then wrote to my friend to say that I had arrived, and would he kindly send or call for me. There was no answer that night, but early the next morning a gentleman and a carriage with two horses came for me and I was very glad, for I thought I would be lost if no one came. We drove off to a railway station, and we went down many steps in a dark tunnel lit up with many lamps. The train came, and we got in and went off under the streets of London. When the train stopped we got out and went up many steps, and then we got into the streets of the city; and oh, what a noise and commotion: I was startled. The streets were filled with carriages, omnibuses, tramway cars, horses and carts of all kinds and sizes, and so close together that we could not pass through them. Thousands of them came on and on without end. And the sides of the streets are just as thronged with people, many thousands, all walking fast, and pushing and crushing that they would knock you down by coming against you if you were not careful and watchful. We pressed our way amongst and through them until we came to my friend's office in Watling Street.

My business kept me till six o'clock in the evening, when I had to return; but I was not going back by the same way that I came in the morning, for my friend had engaged apartments for me at Finsbury

Square. So the gentleman who was directing me took me to see a very wonderful clock, such as I had never seen or thought of before. The clock is erected on the top of a very high house and it has four faces to tell the time; above the clock faces there are large bells, and behind them four men, made of metal, stand ready with their arms uplifted, and hammers in their hands, to strike the hours. One of the faces shows the time in England, the second in Egypt, the third in America, and the fourth in Africa. It was five minutes to the hour and there was a large crowd of people gathered, all looking up. I stopped, and asked, what was the matter? Then my friend explained about it and whilst he was speaking, the hour arrived, and the men, with their hammers, struck the large bells that gave out a loud and pleasant sound.

Having arrived at my lodgings, my friend bade me good-bye and I went in and had my tea, and I took it with ease, and spent much time about it, so that I began to think it was time to go bed, but it was not dark, the sun was still in the heavens. I then read and lounged about. On looking at my watch I saw it was nine o'clock. "What a curious country this is!" I said; "there seems to be no night. In my home in Africa the night begins to come on always, all the year round, by five o'clock, and it is quite dark at six;

but now it is half-past ten, and the day is not entirely gone."

On the following morning it was arranged to take me to see St. Paul's Cathedral. We walked along through the crowded streets until we came to a large square; and in it, and almost filling it, but just leaving a road right around it, was a very large chapel. I was quite astonished when I saw it; I could not take it all in with my eye at the first. My friend, who was always watching me to see if I noticed things, looked curiously at me, and then he said, "This is St. Paul's Cathedral, the largest in England." There were steps all round it, leading to the entrance doors. So we went up into the first hall, which is exceedingly wide and large. There I saw long rows of chair seats, marked A, B, C, to Z. The front of the pulpit contains 100 chairs, marked A; the left side 100 chairs, marked B; the right side 100 chairs, marked C; and thus they continue in hundreds until they come to Z.

The service was very grand. There was a number of men and boys, called choristers, or singers, all arrayed in white robes together with about twenty-four aged ministers, some of them being very old, and who also wear white garments, and they all have to attend to the services, and worship morning and evening the Almighty God.

"Who are these arrayed in white,
　　Brighter than the noonday sun?
Foremost of the sons of light!
　　Nearest the Eternal Throne.

"These are they who bore the Cross,
　　Nobly for the Master stood;
Sufferers in His righteous cause,
　　Followers of the dying Lord.

"Out of great distress they came,
　　Washed their robes by faith below
In the blood of yonder Lamb,
　　Blood that washes white as snow.

"Therefore are they next the Throne,
　　Serve their Maker day and night;
God resides amongst His own, –
　　God does in his saints delight."

We sat down to worship with them, for my soul
was thirsting for the living God, and the time went
very quickly past. The service consists in reading
portions of the Bible that are arranged for the day,
chanting the Psalms, reading prayers and singing
hymns accompanied with the powerful organ, that
almost speaks the words in many tones, which are

changed by the stops, sometimes loud and swelling, and at other times soft and low.

After the service, we were then allowed by the door-keeper to go inside and see the pictures and the monuments, and the statues or marble figures of St. Paul, St. Peter and St. John, with many other modern and beloved men, as well as captains and commanders in the army and navy who died in the wars.

After that, another guide came and took us up many stairs to see the galleries. One is called the whispering gallery; and if you go and put your face to the wall and speak very low in a whisper, it can be heard away off at the other end quite plainly. We then went up hundreds of steps to the second gallery, and then still upwards to the third, where we saw the large clocks and the bells. There is still a fourth gallery, which leads to the dome of the Cathedral. There is a walk all round on the outside, with rails to keep you safe; and from this outside gallery you can see all the great city of London, and far beyond. But I declined to go there for already my legs began to shake as if I had gone too far. So we descended again until we reached the street. Here I noticed a carriage, with a large cask on it, drawn by a large, fat horse, the back of the cask was an iron pipe going across, and holes in it right along. Whilst I was looking, the man sitting in front pulled a string, and all the water shot out of the iron pipe at the back, and came down like rain on the streets. I said to my companion, "What is that man and his horse trying to do, wetting all the streets like that?" He said, "Did you never see that before? That is to keep the dust from blowing into our eyes and dirtying our clothes."

As I passed along the streets, I noticed the people looking at me very earnestly. The small boys especially would stand and stare, and would sometimes call out to me, "Holloa! blacky, can't you wash your face before you come out in the morning, and make it white?" my companion kindly said, "You must not take notice of them, because they do not know any better."

The next morning, my kind friend came again for me at my lodgings, and we went to see the Thames Embankment, a long, strong wall built alongside the river. We there saw Cleopatra's Needle, a long upright monument made of marble, and lately brought from Egypt. He then went into the Houses of Parliament, but the members were not there; and we crossed the road and went into Westminster Abbey, which is a grand church, where they bury the kings and queens and all the great men of England. Their monuments are all round on the walls, and are very interesting. We also visited Buckingham Palace, one of the residences of the Queen; and Marlborough House the residence of the Prince of Wales; and closed a heavy day's work by going to Madame Tussaud's wax-work exhibition. All the figures were dressed up like living men and women. The following day was entirely spent in the Crystal Palace, a very large collection of buildings all covered in by glass roofs. The inside is full of wonders; so many that I am bewildered when I think of them and I really cannot describe them. There were all kinds of machines working away as if they were in a factory. I stayed all the day looking first at one thing and then another, and yet they said I had not seen half of what there was in. At nine o'clock we all went outside of the building to see the fireworks, which appeared to me very curious, grand, and frightful. Altogether I was eight days in London, and everyday I was out seeing some grand thing, until I got as tired as if I had been on a long, weary journey.

London is a very great place; I thought far too big and confusing, and I would not like to stay there. I was glad therefore, to come back to Liverpool and be quiet.

My friends in Liverpool are very kind to me, and often ask me to their private houses. I went with one friend, and he introduced me to his family, one little boy and two girls. During the evening one of the little girls, about six years of age, came and said to me, "Mr. Ocansey, I wish when you go back to Africa that you would send your little black boy here, and then he could carry my books to school for me." The father said, "Wary, my love, what are you saying? Suppose I give you to Mr. Ocansey, and he will take you to Africa, and then you will have to carry the books for the black boy?" She looked round smart, and said, "But I shall not go to Africa, the sun will make me a black girl, and you said that they have no good schools in Africa."

On another occasion, as I was going with a friend to his home, we had to go down a street loading to the docks, when a poor white boy came and ran along with us, and sometimes before us, begging for a penny. He looked so beseechingly, and begged so strongly, that I said to him, "What is it you want?" He said, "A penny, please!" And I was just going to give him one when my friend said, "No! do not do it; you encourage begging, and we want to put it down; for no one in England need beg in the street if they are honest and willing to work." But the boy still followed us, and he looked so miserable that I gave him a penny, and then he left us with his thanks.

My friend now explained to me that every man who lives in a house in England is taxed every year to keep the poor, and the sick, and the cripples in a large house called a workhouse, and that when that is too full they give 1s., 2s., or 3s. or more per week to the poor people to keep them in their own houses. And he said they that follow you and beg are idle and very bad, and ought not to be helped, for they spend it in strong drink, and the parents of those ragged children are somewhere near, and take the money from them.

The Sunday mornings in Liverpool are very pleasant to me. There are a great many churches, with beautiful sweet bells, and these all commence to ring and mix their sounds on the Sabbath morning, and they are sweet music to me, and make me long to worship God.

"While in joyful chorus
    Chime the Sabbath bells,
Let us seek the temple
    Where our Father dwells;
Bonding there before Him,
    Ask for grace divine,
Light of hope eternal,
    In our hearts to shine.

"Welcome day, holy day,
Hear the passing moments gently say,

'Watch and pray, watch and pray,
Come to Jesus, come away.'

"Day of rest from labour,
        Pure and tranquil rest;
Day of sweet refreshing,
        By our Father blest.
May our soul's devotion
        Kindle while we sing
Praise to Him who made it,
        Praise to God our King!

"Welcome day, holy day,
Hear the passing moments gently say,
'Watch and pray, watch and pray,
Come to Jesus, come away.'"

When I knew that the trial in which I was concerned would be delayed until the end of July, I felt depressed as to what I should do in the interval to fill up my time. I thought I should be killed by idleness, or lost for something to do. But every day I find too short to do what I would like; and my English friends say they will teach me to combine business with pleasure. But I say it is all pleasure, and not business to me.

One day I arranged to visit Manchester with my

friend Mr. Wood, of the firm of Messrs. Edwards Brothers, and we went on the same railway that took me to London, but after we had gone on the line for some distance, there was a parting in the rails which branched off to Manchester, and we ran on them, and got from Liverpool to Manchester in forty-five minutes. When we came near to the city, I looked out of the window, and I saw that the railway was very high up on large arches above the houses, and that we looked down on their roofs and on their chimneys. All about, for a very long distance, there were great, tall, brick-built chimneys standing up like a forest of trees, but all sending out clouds of black smoke and steam. I thought the people would have to hold their breath such dense, thick, black smoke, same as our people do when they go down in the water; but when I left the carriages, and got into the city, I found no smell of smoke – all was pleasant.

At twelve o'clock at noon I was in the streets, when I heard a great many bells ringing; and I looked about to see if there was fire somewhere. Then the gates of the factories opened quickly, and there was a great crowd of people running and pushing with all their might to get out, and then I concluded the fire must be there, and that they are escaping for their lives, and I think I shall have to run too; but I enquired what was the matter, and I was told, "Oh, it is only meal-hour," or dinner-time; all the people were going "chop," as we say in Africa, for one hour. Manchester is also a very large city; as large, I am told, as Liverpool, but the people are not so much in the streets – they work in the mills and factories.

After our business was done, we went to see the Zoological Gardens, which are about two miles from the city. It was a new and strange sight to me - it was wonderland! The gardens were beautifully laid out, and then there was a large collection of wild living birds and beasts, such as I had never seen before. We had to pay at the gate to get admission into the gardens, but afterwards we could walk about wherever we pleased. All the birds and the wild beasts were in large cages with strong iron bars, and men called keepers are appointed to look after them, and to feed them. You have to buy a small book as you enter, called a guide; and it tells you the name of everything in the gardens, and where you can find them. The book showed us that there were 164 cages to be seen. Some of the animals were like what I had seen in Africa, but most of them were new and strange to me and came from England, and from far-off countries. We came to a large house in the gardens, and it was called the elephant house, and there I saw two large Indian Elephants. I was greatly pleased with their size and with their wisdom. They moved their long trunks about from one side to another amongst the people as though they were begging or asking for something. And the people, and sometimes little children, gave them biscuits, which they quickly twisted into their large mouths; and sometimes they got money, and put it into a box, but the money slipped down beside the man who sold the biscuits, and he gave the elephants the number of biscuits the money would buy, and they knew how many they should have, and would wait for and insist on the right number. I was also greatly pleased with the seals from the Polar seas. They have faces like a dog, with large sparkling eyes, and very smooth, hairy, glossy skins. They dive down in the water, and keep down a long time, and then when they pop up they can spring on to the rocks prepared for them, and move about with their flappers, which are like feet. The keepers buy dead fish for them and throw them into the water, but the seals watch them coming and catch them as they touch the water, they are so quick. I was well pleased with what I saw, but it would take a long time to look carefully at everything; besides, we were hurried to see the grand fireworks, which were very wonderful.

On another day, my friend Mr. M. Merschell arranged for me to go to Southport, which is about twenty miles from Liverpool. Starting from the Exchange Station we reached it in one hour. I was told that but a few years since all the land was wild sandhills, but they have been cleared away, and a beautiful large town is now built, and many families from Liverpool, Manchester and other towns come to live here for their health; for there are no factories and no smoke, therefore abundance of pure air. Many thousands of people will come in the railway trains in the morning and remain but one day to refresh themselves, and then go home at night. The streets are all very wide, clean and straight; and the houses facing the sea are very high and have many rooms, which are hired and paid for by the strangers that come to stay a short time for their pleasure. The way in which the town lies on the banks of the river Mersey brought to my recollection part of West Africa, say from Addah to Argrarvay; but here at Southport there were no trees and bushes by the river side as there are in Africa. But the place is very pretty indeed, and there is a long pier, or stage, supported on iron pillars, running far into the sea. There is a little railway on this stage, or pier, and you can ride upon it, or you can walk down; and if you feel it is too long you can sit down on the wooden benches, or in the little shelter houses. When the tide goes back then a large part of the beach is bare and dry; and the people bring out horses and donkeys for hire, and very little children, and boys and girls, as well as men and women, pay their money and have great fun in taking a ride. I saw also that they had boats mounted on four wheels, and the people pay twopence and climb into them. Then the sails are hoisted, and the wind makes them run on the dry sand just like as if they were in the water! There were also steam launches to take the people out to sea on pleasure, for sixpence.

The beach and the river side were crowded with people out enjoying themselves, and it seemed to me very gay and pleasant. There was also plenty of music.

After we had been on the beach a long time, we came back into the town, and again I was greatly pleased to see the very long streets, and to notice the beautiful, sweet flowers that were growing in the little gardens in front of the houses. There is a grand building, covered in with glass roofs, and warmed by iron pipes, through which hot water is forced. It is called the "Winter Gardens," because in the winter time in England, when all the trees are bare, and all the ground barren and covered with snow, inside of this building, or garden, all the African flowers and trees are in full bloom, and the people come in and are warmed, and enjoy the beautiful sight. Southport is not a trade town like Liverpool or Manchester, but a town of pleasure and refreshment for the summer time. Many gentlemen come from it to Liverpool for business every day, and I saw some of them arrange themselves in parties of four and play cards, and I thought railway travelling is indeed very pleasant; for in Africa, when a man is travelling, where can he put his heavy load down and play cards, and still be travelling?

On returning, my friend asked me to go with him to his home, and we were walking up the streets of Everton Valley, when I saw a crowd of people gathered together looking at something on the ground. I pushed in amongst them, and then I saw a man who had taken too much drink, or spirits, and he could not stand up or walk; and the policeman came and pulled him up and dragged him to the lock-up, or jail, until the morning, when he would then be brought before the magistrates; and it was still they would fine him five shillings and costs for being drunk. Well, I thought, I have been here two months, and I have seen many thousands of English people, and this is the only one I have seen drunk and incapable; whereas, if I had been in Africa, I could see a dozen or more men drunk every day. Yes, in Africa we have too much drink, and that is one thing we must try to cure, or else our people will not rise to be a great people.

The street cries of Liverpool have puzzled and amused me very much. One morning I heard quite an alarm and loud shouting. I jumped up from the breakfast table, and said, "Now, there is a row and so early in the morning." But when I looked out I saw two strong, stout old women, with large baskets on their heads, shouting with all their strength something that did not appear to me as English, but as my native tongue, and I thought they said Muhoohoo and sung it loud and long. But the door of the house opposite opened, and the servant looked out, and the women were watching for someone to buy, and they saw her, and went and put down their baskets at her feet on the steps, and then I saw that one basket was full of fish, and the other of vegetables, which they wanted to sell.

A few days after I had been in Liverpool, and was walking down the streets, a small boy ran up to me, and touched his cap to salute me. I thought, perhaps, he knew me. He then pointed down to my boots, and I looked down too, for I began to be uneasy, thinking there was something wrong with my feet; but the boy continued touching his cap and pointing to my boots, and crying out "Shine sir." "Shine, sir; only a penny." Then I saw he had blacking and brushes, and a little stand to rest the foot on; and he wanted to earn a penny by blacking my boots!

In the afternoons, and evenings especially, quite a large number of small boys and girls are in the streets selling newspapers. And they are very quick, and watch every person going up or down the street to see if they will buy one. Now I like the newspaper. It is a luxury to me as it is to the white man. It is very cheap, and contains much information from all parts, and about many things. Then I thought I would buy one, and I put my hand in my pocket to see if I had a copper. Instantly the boys and girls detected my intention, and half-a-dozen came bounding towards me, and thrusting their papers at me, said, "Please buy from me." "Please take mine; I saw you first!" and I could hardly get away from them.

On the 14th of July, the African steamer "Lual-aba," arrived in Liverpool from the West Coast of Africa; and I learned on looking over the names of the passengers that Mr. Christian Jacobson, of Quitta, was a passenger on board. Mr. Jacobson is the companion of my youth, my best friend, and a relative of the Ocansey family. I lost no time, there-fore, in going down to the steamer but all the passengers had gone ashore, and gone away into the city. So I had to begin to enquire all about "where had Mr. Jacobson gone to?" and at last I found him at the Alexandra Hotel, Dale Street. And he had been making many enquiries after me, so that when we saw each other we were glad indeed, and thanked God together for His journeying mercies and kind protection. And now with my friend's presence, I began to feel quite at home and comfortable, for he came to my lodgings to live with me, and he tells me all the latest news of my family. He is the first native of Quitta who has visited Europe. May he be the forerunner of many hundreds:

After our first salutations were over, then, to my great sorrow, I learned that he had come on a similar miserable business as myself, namely, to try to recover a bad debt.

It appears that Mr. Jacobson had been trading with Messrs. Taylor & Co., of 72, Virginia Street, Glasgow, and had consigned to them African produce to the value of £183. Immediately after they had received the produce and realised cash for it, than the firm failed, without sending Mr. Jacobson money or goods. But they wrote a letter to him saying that they had an account due to them by some people in Grand Bassar, on the Coast of Africa, and that if Mr. Jacobson could get that account he might pay himself; and, if he could not, then they would give it into the hands of their agents at Sierra Leone, and, if they got it, then Mr. Jacobson should be paid! Now, Mr. Jacobson is a young man just venturing out into trade; and it does seem very cruel that he should meet with such heartless conduct, and suffer so great a loss, on the doorstep of his life. To ask him, who lives at Quitta, to collect another man's account from the people at Grand Bassar, is adding insult to injury. It takes the main steamer sixteen days to go from Quitta to Grand Bassar: and the Quitta people have no dealings with them. Mr. Jacobson was advised by his friends to go with the steamer to Sierra Leone, and there see the agents of Messrs. Taylor & Co. who would know more about the account, and the likelihood of obtaining it from the people indebted. But when he called upon them they said they could not help him, for at Grand Bassar there was no British protection, and if they went or sent to demand the debt they would be sure to be killed or robbed: So Mr. Jacobson came on to England, and he wrote to Messrs. Taylor & Co. to say that he had arrived and that he would call upon them for his account. But they sent a letter back at once, saying that they had nothing to do with their past affairs; that they had paid a part or composition to those who would receive it and as to his account they still expected it would be got from the people of Grand Bassar, and they could say no more as to that matter, but if Mr. Jacobson would send them any more produce they would do well for him: This letter came to him from Glasgow to Liverpool on Monday evening, and when it was read we both sorrowed greatly, and could not go out to fulfil an invitation. He has not only lost his £183, but he has paid £54 for his return ticket, and loses his valuable time, and receives a deep wound in his trading experience that will fill him with suspicions all his life. White men who act so unrighteously do a great injury to their race, for we are afraid to send our goods to them; and in trying to protect ourselves we have to give a deal of trouble even to the honest and straightforward merchant. But we must commit our ways to the Lord, and pray that if we have to suffer so much by the loss of our worldly goods, He would recompense us in some other way and give to us the spirit of resignation which Job had when he lost all, and could say: "For we brought nothing into this world, and it is certain we can carry nothing out;" "and having food and raiment let us therewith be content" "Yea, blessed be the name of the Lord."

Some of my friends in Liverpool have great faith in Africa, and they say they are sure Africa will be one of the great countries of the future. "And who knows," they say to me, "but what God in his providence and wisdom may call <u>you</u> to take some humble part in hastening on the chariot wheels? therefore prepare yourself by observation and experience to encourage your people." And so they take me about to see how the English people do their business and take their pleasure. I have been through the markets on the Saturday mornings, when the stalls have been filled with butchers' meat, and all kinds of fowls, and fruits, and flowers, and vegetables; for all these things are now in their prime, it being summer time; and a large business is being carried on, for the markets are crowded with people. I have also been to one of the newspaper offices, and seen the large and wonderful machine that prints the paper and cuts and folds them at the same time.

On Sunday afternoon, July 17th, I was asked, along with Jacobson, to attend a preaching service in the open air. It was said that it was an old English custom to preach in the open air and that it was greatly prized by many, but that other people did not care for it. "But if you come you will see many English people who do not attend church or chapel, but who have got into bad ways and drink too much. Still, the gospel is for them, and they ought to hear it, and if they will not come to us we must go to them. And besides, we want you to see the dark side of English life as well as the bright." So I went, and was much pleased with the earnest addresses that were given. There were, I thought, nearly 1,000 persons standing about Gill-street market, and they listened very attentively, and sang some of the hymns. But I saw they were not like the regular chapel-people, some of the men who lived near came out without their coats or hats on, smoking their pipes; and there were many women with babies, but no Sunday clothes on, and I saw many of them wipe the tears from their eyes as they listened to the speakers.

There was a coloured man there, who seemed to be well known by every one, and especially by the small boys, who made very free with him, calling him "Abraham." Seeing us present, he looked quite pleased, and came smiling up to us, and said that he came from New York, America, and that his people (the coloured people) have fine chapels there. He wanted to have a great deal of talk, but I did not feel towards him, for as I looked at his dirty dress and his face, I thought "you do not live a good life." I asked about him after the service, and they told me he was a "knocker-up," and they explained it by saying that he lives by going out early every morning and knocking loudly at the doors of people who have to get up and go to their business, and they pay him so much per week. After the service we went for tea to the house of that mother to all black boys, Mrs. Looney, and there were many friends with us. After tea they were very anxious for me and Mr. Jacobson to sing together so he played the piano, and we sang a hymn in English, and then I played, and we sang a hymn in our native language. Then the friends all sang, and we had a most enjoyable time.

Although sight-seeing was extremely interesting and instructive to me, I always felt some sensation of the miserable business that had brought me to England. There were times when this depression of feeling came over me like a thick, black cloud and I could not raise myself above it. I would not come down into the city because I felt I could not mix up in any society with any pleasure. So I remained all day in my lodgings, and very long days and nights they were. And to be true and faithful, I must confess I began to be home-sick, and impatient of every hour's delay that separated me from my home and friends. And what had I to expect from this wretched trial? There was no money to recover. In some foolish or mysterious way Hickson had either spent or lost all our money; and now our only consolation was that we should uphold the power of the law, and punish a dishonest, fraudulent man. However, I was glad the time was drawing near when we should be done with it, and having come to and known the bitter end, we might start afresh, and endeavour to regain our lost ground in the great battle of life.

THE ASSIZE COURT AND ITS SURROUNDINGS

On the morning of the 27th I was at St. George's Hall before ten o'clock. There was a large crowd of people gathered all around and standing on the steps. I was told that most of them were people who had cases in the court and their witnesses, and the jurymen, and the solicitors, and their clerks, &c. At ten o'clock a very handsome carriage came down the street and stopped at the door of the large London and North-Western Hotel, opposite to the hall. The carriage was drawn by four very splendid horses, and their harness was all ornamented with gold. The driver, who was an aged, stout man, was grandly dressed in livery, with a three square cocked hat; and two men, dressed in the same way, and holding a white stick in one hand, stood on a small platform at the end of the carriage, holding on by a strap.

The people then ran and surrounded the entrance to the hotel, to get a sight of the judge as he came down to get into his carriage. About twenty or thirty men, dressed in large cloth coats of a light colour, trimmed with yellow, and with long pikes in their hands, guarded and kept a clear space at the doorway. There were also three men, dressed in livery, with silver trumpets, and as soon as they caught a sight of the judge descending the steps, they began to play. The judge wore a black gown faced with a broad band of scarlet cloth, and had a large powdered wig on his head. He hurried into the carriage, which then drove off to the entrance of the court at the end of the large hall, which is but a short distance from the hotel, where he gets out and walks along the large, wide lobby to his room. An officer, with a white stick or wand, goes before him, and the trumpeters play outside on the steps, and the music, soft and harmonious, can be distinctly heard in the court, which is now filled with people. The court is in the form of a half circle. The judge sits in a large chair on a platform. Immediately below him are the officers who have charge of and prepare all the business, calling out the names of the prisoners, and swearing in the jury, &c. Then next to them there are two rows of barristers, who wear black gowns and have wigs on their heads. Just behind them is the dock, or the place where the prisoners have to stand whilst their trial is going on, which is railed round and guarded by police officers.

The prisoners are brought up into this dock from the cells below. The clerk then begins to call out a large number of names of jurymen who have been summoned. Each name is written on a small white card, and when the person hears his name called out he rises and says "Here." If any one does not answer his name, the card is put on one side and he is fined. When he has called out all the names he then begins again and selects twelve men, and these go into seats prepared for them at the left-hand side of the judge. As soon as they are all in and have taken their seats, another man rises and tells them to take the bible in their hands, and they are sworn in; and after that no one but the judge or the barristers dare speak to them, and that must be in the open court.

The folding doors are then thrown open, and the judge enters and as he does so every person in the court rises and makes a bow to him, which he returns. And these ceremonies are repeated every morning as long as the Assizes last.

Besides the jury I have named who have to decide in open court on the cases argued before them, there is a Grand Jury composed of twenty-four merchants and gentlemen. These sit in a large room by themselves, with barristers to assist and advise them. After waiting about until noon, I was called in before these gentlemen, and I saw all our letters and documents on the table before them. I was called upon and sworn, and they asked me a few questions. Then they called for the person who should have built the steam launch, and then for the broker who sold our goods; and after they had spoken to each other for a little time, they returned a true bill against Hickson, and told me to appear in court next day at ten o'clock in the morning.

I was told that this grand jury was necessary to examine every case to see that the charges against the prisoners were proper and lawful, to make sure that the prosecutor and the witnesses were present, and that everything was right and in order before it came before the judge in open court. They thus save his time and prevent confusion and interruption.

On the following day I went down as directed; but the first case called upon was one for murder, and I was told it would take all day. So I was set free. Again, on the Saturday, I was at the court at its opening, and had to remain till noon, when I was told it would not come on that day, but would be tried on the Monday. On the Monday I was in attendance, and some of the officers said it would be certain to come on to-day, but others said it would not. However, a little after noon, we were told it would not, and that we might go, and that on the following day a great trial was coming on about two men who had attempted to blow up the Liverpool Town Hall, and very likely it would occupy the whole of the day. As I did not feel well, it was arranged that I should remain all day in my lodgings, and if I was wanted an officer would come up for me with a cab. But I was not wanted. On the Wednesday morning I went down to the opening of the court, and some of the officers were certain my case would be brought on that day; and so we had to wait about till past noon, when we were told it was postponed till the morning. On the Thursday, as soon as the court opened, the clerk called out for Robert William Hickson. He was not in the court, but a gentleman said "He is in the lobby" (for he was out on bail, and had his liberty), and a policeman went into the lobby and called for him and he came into court, and the policeman opened the door of the dock to admit him as a prisoner: but just as he was entering, his wife, who was sitting quite near the door of the dock, rose and gave him a kiss.

During all the days we had been attending court, we had seen Hickson several times walking about and speaking with his barristers. Some of his friends at the first said they were sure he would get off free from punishment, for there was no fraud in the transaction, it was only an ordinary failure in business, and that if he did get acquitted, then he would commence an action against us for false imprisonment, and we would have to suffer. It was said he had secured the services of the cleverest barrister in Liverpool Mr. J.B. Aspinall, Recorder of the City, to plead for him. But in a day or two we found that Hickson's friends had changed their tune for Mr. Aspinall, having looked into his case, told him plainly he could not be defended, and that the best thing he could do was to plead guilty, and claim the merciful sentence of the judge. Mr. Aspinall then spoke to our counsel, Mr. Carver, and told him what he had advised Hickson to do, and he pleaded hard for him. Mr. Carver told him it was a very serious thing for us and for all merchants and that if such cases were allowed to go unpunished it would slur the confidence of all persons engaged in trade. But at the same time we did not wish to be vindictive or revengeful; our case was prepared and we must go on with it. Mr. Aspinall, on behalf of the prisoner, acknowledged all; still there were many extenuating circumstances that might excite the merciful consideration of the court. He would take the evidence as true and conclusive and therefore we need not go through it in open court, and here he would simply make some observations in favour of a slight sentence to the prisoner. And this was agreed to, and the trial proceeded.

Published 1881

W. E. B. Du Bois

Dr W. E. B. Du Bois (1868–1963) is recognized as the foremost African American scholar–activist of the twentieth century. Throughout his long life he was an eminent historian and sociologist, as well as a leading figure in the Civil Rights and Pan-African movements. He was a prolific writer, particularly well known for seminal texts such as *The Souls of Black Folk* (1903) and *Black Reconstruction* (1935) that are still widely read today. He was one of the founders of the National Association for the Advancement of Colored People and for many years the editor of its official magazine *The Crisis*. He is also notable for his leading role in the Niagara Movement, for convening four Pan-African Congresses in the period following World War I, and for his peace campaigning and persecution by the US government during the Cold War. The extract here was written following his visit to London to attend the Universal Races Congress in 1911.

London

There is in the world no city like London. Nor is its distinction merely a matter of size. To be sure, it is a vast aggregation of men—it gives the visitor a curious sense of endlessness by its very disorganization, by the fact that one can find center after center of busy running life stretching away mile after mile and yet all is London. London has no beauty that will compare it to Paris, no blare and flare like New York.

Yet London has an individuality, a tradition and an importance that make it the capital of the world in a sense, true of no other center since the days of imperial Rome. The individuality is peculiar, subtle, striking—yet difficult to express. One sees a busy mart of endless interests, world-wide ramifications, tremendous power. One sees a tradition, a memory clothed in living flesh and word, and a power which makes this city an expression of the empire on which the sun never sets.

This empire is a colored empire. Most of its subjects—a vast majority of its subjects—are colored people. And more and more the streets of London are showing this fact. I seldom step into the streets without meeting a half dozen East Indians, a Chinaman, a Japanese or a Malay, and here and there a Negro. There must be thousands of colored people in the city. They do not, of course, color the world so obviously as in an American city, but one senses continually the darker world.

No pageant to-day in London is complete without the colored representatives. In the two great coronation processions it was the black and brown and yellow Indian princes in the brilliant magnificence of their silk and jewels who shared the plaudits of the crowds with the king himself, and the black Prince of Abyssinia rode among the royal guests.

London is polite and considerate to her darker brothers. There is color prejudice and aloofness undoubtedly here, but it does not parade its shame like New York or its barbarity like New Orleans. Hotel, theater and restaurant stand not only open, but studiously attentive and polite. The courtesies of the street and the tramcar are thoughtfully passed, and in the highest social life colored men and women at the last days of festivity sat at the tables of the highest in the land.

Yet London is uneasy. London is sensing the strength and determination in the darker world and is wondering what it all portends in the future. The unrest in India and Egypt causes deep and widespread apprehension in all England, and the situation in South Africa is being narrowly watched.

What more fitting center then than London for the coming together of the first world conference of the races and peoples of the world! They are to meet not as master and slave, missionary and heathen, conqueror and conquered—but as men and equals in the center of the world, and the meeting will be watched with intense interest and remembered for many a long day.

Published 1911

MACMILLAN COLLECTOR'S LIBRARY

Own the world's great works of literature in one beautiful collectible library

Designed and curated to appeal to book lovers everywhere, Macmillan Collector's Library editions are small enough to travel with you and striking enough to take pride of place on your bookshelf. These much-loved literary classics also make the perfect gift.

Beautifully produced with gilt edges, a ribbon marker, bespoke illustrated cover and real cloth binding, every Macmillan Collector's Library hardback adheres to the same high production values.

Discover something new or cherish your favourite stories with this elegant collection.

Macmillan Collector's Library: own, collect, and treasure

Discover the full range at
macmillancollectorslibrary.com